THE KILLING NEEDLE

D1521149

THE KILLING NEEDLE

Henry Cauvain

Translated by John Pugmire

The Killing Needle

This book is a work of fiction. The characters, incidents, and dialogue are drawn from the author's imagination and are not to be construed as real. Any resemblance to actual events or persons, living or dead, is entirely coincidental.

First published in French in 1871 by
J. Lecoffre as *Maximilien Heller* and later as *l'Aiguille qui tue*
English translation copyright © by John Pugmire 2014.

For information, contact: pugmire1@yahoo.com

FIRST AMERICAN EDITION
Library of Congress Cataloging-in-Publication Data
Cauvain, Henry
[*L'Aiguille qui tue*. English]
The Killing Needle / Henry Cauvain
Translated from the French by John Pugmire

FOREWORD

L'Aiguille qui tue (The Killing Needle), originally entitled *Maximilien Heller*, first appeared in 1871, sixteen years before Sherlock Holmes made his bow. It was the first of twelve novels by Henry Cauvain (1847-1899) who, despite the English spelling of his forename, was born in Paris to French parents. This translation is based on the 1930 Librarie Hachette edition of *L'Aiguille qui tue* which differs from the original *Maximilien Heller* only in the chapter structure.

Messrs. Lacourbe, Bourgeois, Fooz and Soupart, writing about Cauvain in their classic bibliography *1001 Chambres Closes (Semper Aenigma, 2013)* state: "His detective foreshadows Sherlock Holmes…Like Holmes he is an amateur chemist, has misanthropic tendencies, is a master of disguise and is adept at deductive reasoning." They might have added that Heller's exploits, like those of Holmes, were notable for their audacity.

Celebrated French literary critic Michel Lebrun writes: "Heller is fond of cats, like Holmes. If Holmes dopes himself with heroin, Heller does opium. Like Holmes, he practices rigorous logical reasoning. Like Holmes, he has a friend and confidant, the narrator of the story." (Jean Tulard, *Dictionnaire du roman policier, Fayard, 2005*).

Claude Mesplède, French detective fiction expert, writes, in *Dictionnaire des Litteratures Policières (Joseph K.,2003)*: "Heller is a neurotic misanthrope …The fact that the hero takes drugs, is a master of deductive reasoning and has a doctor as his confidant, might lead one to suspect the author had plagiarised the Sherlock of Conan Doyle. Not a bit of it. The work was published sixteen years before the first appearance of the famous British detective."

French-language Wikipedia states unequivocally that "the personage of Maximilien Heller, in the novel of the same name, published in 1871, was adopted by Arthur Conan Doyle to create that of Sherlock Holmes."

This view is not shared by English-language Wikipedia, which claims that: "Joseph Bell…is perhaps best known as an inspiration for the literary character Sherlock Holmes… Arthur Conan Doyle met Bell in 1877, and served as his clerk at the Edinburgh Royal Infirmary. Doyle later went on to write a series of popular stories featuring Sherlock Holmes, who Doyle stated was loosely based on Bell and his observant ways."

All well and good, and certainly Bell was a master of deductive reasoning and contemporary forensics and chemistry, but was he a misanthropic, drug-taking master of disguise? Were his audacious exploits recorded by a doctor who was a friend and confidant? These are trademarks of the Holmes canon, and correspond exactly to Maximilien Heller (except that Heller did not play the violin.) And Heller appeared in print six years before Doyle even met Bell.

We know that Doyle read French and was not averse to using material from continental sources. As pointed out by S.S. Van Dine in a footnote in *The Greene Murder Case*, "The Problem of Thor Bridge" matched almost exactly the real life circumstances surrounding the death of Austrian grain merchant "A.M.," as described on pages 834-836 of volume II of *Hans Gross's Handbook for Examining Magistrates, Police Officials and Military Policemen, etc.* published in 1893, almost thirty years before Thor Bridge.

So, was Maximilien Heller at least partly the inspiration for Sherlock Holmes? There seem to be too many coincidences for that not to be the case.

Little else is known about Henry Cauvain, except that he was Treasurer of the Eure region of France during the IIIrd Republic.
His first book, a milestone in detective fiction of whatever language, was written when he was only twenty-four years old.

John Pugmire

PART I

1

It was on the third of January 1845, at eight o'clock in the evening, that I first made the acquaintance of Monsieur Maximilien Heller.

Several days before, I had been approached in the street by one of my friends, Jules H…, who, once the preliminary courtesies had been exchanged, had said to me in particularly urgent tones:

'I've been wanting to visit you for quite some time, my dear doctor, in the hope that you could do me a great service. One of my old colleagues at the Bar, M. Heller, who lives close by, is in a quite alarming state of health. My friends and I had initially thought the cause to be more moral than physical. We tried every distraction we could think of, and we went to great lengths to try and raise his spirits and stimulate his intelligence, which has always hitherto been of a blinding clarity. I must admit all our efforts have been in vain. Our only remaining choice is to turn to science for help. What our friendship has failed to achieve, your authority as a doctor perhaps will. Maximilien is of a forceful nature and will, I believe, only submit to a higher reason. If you would pay him a visit one of these evenings, my dear friend, and see what you can do for the poor fellow, I should be particularly grateful for it.'

The following week, in accordance with my friend's wishes, and even though I was loath to do so – for I had heard talk of Maximilien Heller being a disagreeable eccentric, and sullen to boot – I dropped in on my new patient. He lived in one of those streets winding up St. Roch hill.

The house was very narrow – the façade was only two windows wide – but, on the other hand, it was disproportionately high. It consisted of five storeys and two mansard roofs stacked one on top of the other. On the ground floor, a green painted fruit shop opened on to the street.

A low door with a wire grille on the upper part led to the interior of the house. After traversing a long, dark, corridor whose parquet yielded underfoot, I came suddenly upon a pair of worm-eaten steps, invisible in the darkness, against which I inevitably stumbled.

The noise of the fall alerted the concierge to the presence of a visitor in the building. It was certainly a most ingenious method of saving the cost of a doorbell.

I was still smarting from the disagreeable experience of stubbing my toe in the dark when I heard a shrill voice like that of a witch emanate from a small space beneath the stairs.

'What do you want? Where are you going?' cried the invisible Cerberus.

'Is M. Maximilien Heller at home?' I responded, turning my head in the direction of the voice.

'Sixth floor, door on the right,' replied the disembodied voice, laconically.

I began my laborious ascent.

Either out of ignorance, or just to simplify his task, the architect had not given the stairs their conventional circular form. Instead, they consisted of a series of straight ladders connecting narrow landings, on to which opened the blackened doors of the rooms.

I finally reached the sixth floor. The light at the end of a narrow corridor served to guide me. It came from a small, smoky lamp hanging from a nail near the first door on the right.

'This must be it,' I said to myself. I knocked discreetly.

'Come in,' said a feeble voice.

I pushed open the door, which was secured only by a latch, and went into M. Maximilien Heller's room.

It was a remarkable sight. The walls were bare, but covered in a few places by strips of the most vulgar wallpaper. To the left, a faded rose-coloured curtain hung from a rail, no doubt hiding a bed in the wall recess behind. A fire made from clods of earth burned in the little fireplace. On a table in the middle of the modest cell, papers and books were stacked high in total disarray.

Maximilien Heller lay sprawled in a large armchair in front of the fireplace. His head was thrown back and his feet were resting on the fire dogs. A long greatcoat enveloped his body, which was as thin as a skeleton. In front of him, in the ashes, a little tin hot water bottle gurgled at a cricket in the hearth. Maximilien drank a great deal of coffee.

A fat cat, its claws buried in its furry chest and its eyes half-closed, emitted a monotonous snore. Hearing me enter, the cat got up and arched its back; its master did not stir. He lay still, his eyes staring fixedly on the ceiling, his slender white hands resting on the sides of the armchair.

I was surprised by the welcome and hesitated an instant, then approached the strange personage to inform him of the purpose of my visit.

'Ah! It's you, doctor,' he said, turning his head slightly towards me. 'Someone told me about you. Please have a seat. In fact, do I have a seat to offer you? Ah, yes. I do believe I've got one left. It's over there in the corner.' I collected the chair he had pointed to, and came back to sit next to him.

'Dear old Jules!' he continued. "He thought I was very sick the last time he came to visit, and promised to send over someone from the Faculty.... Are you the Faculty?'

I smiled and nodded.

'Yes, actually, I am suffering quite a bit. For a while now, I've had periods of forgetfulness and I can't stand bright light.....And I'm always cold.'

He leaned his long body forward towards the chimney and stirred the fire with the tongs. The flame that flared up bathed the strange man's face in a red light. He seemed to be no more than thirty years old; but the black rings round his eyes, the pale lips, the greying hair, and the shaking limbs made him seem almost an old man. He shifted awkwardly in the armchair and held out his hand.

'I've got a fever, haven't I?' he asked. His hand was burning, and his pulse was rapid and erratic.

I asked him all the standard questions; he replied in a weak voice and without moving his head. When I had completed my examination, I thought to myself: "This man is lost."

'I'm really sick, aren't I? How much longer do I have to live?' he asked with a penetrating stare.

I didn't answer the awkward question.

'Have you been suffering for a long time?' I asked.

'Oh, yes!' he said with such an emphasis it made my blood run cold. 'Oh, yes!' he repeated, tapping his forehead.

'Would you like me to write you a prescription?'

'Gladly,' he replied, distractedly.

I went over to the table which was, as I said, covered with books and manuscripts and there, by the light of a flickering candle, I dashed off the prescription. Imagine my surprise, when I had finished, to find my patient standing next to me, reading the few scribbled lines with an amused smile on his lips.

He took the paper, studied it for a few moments, then shrugged his shoulders:

'Remedies,' he said, 'always remedies. Do you really think, Monsieur, that they can cure me?'

As he spoke he looked at me with a melancholy stare, then, crumpling it in his hands, he threw the paper in the fire. He leant against the chimney and, taking my hand, spoke in a suddenly gentle voice:

'Forgive the sudden gesture but, my God, you had a great idea there. You're young,' he continued, with his perpetual smile, 'and you believe your medicine to be all-powerful.'

'My dear sir,' I replied rather sharply, 'I believe the best thing for you would be to follow a course of treatment and diet appropriate to your condition.'

'My mental condition, you mean? You think I'm mad, don't you? Well, you're right. In my case, the brain dominates everything and is continually boiling over. This fire is eating me up and doesn't leave me a moment's peace. The mind! The mind is a vulture that's eating me alive.'

'Why don't you try to liberate yourself from its cruel yoke? Why don't you get some rest and something to divert your mind?'

'Remedies, distractions!' he retorted sharply. 'You're all the same. One buys the one at a pharmacy and the other at a box office. That's supposed to cure you. And if it doesn't, you die. But that's never the fault of the Faculty of Medicine.'

2

"Don't you have any parents or friends—?'

He interrupted me again.

'Parents? No... my father died very young, just after I was born. And my poor mother'—and it seemed to me that his voice changed as he pronounced the word—'for twenty years my poor mother worked herself to the bone to bring me up and give me a fine education, and she died from the effort. And how's this for irony? A week after her death I inherited a tidy sum from an old uncle I never knew existed. Friends? I have a few. Jules, for one, who is a fine fellow although he laughs too much and that makes me sick. And all the others who are concerned for me and who recommended me into your care. They think me mad as well, and when I'm amongst them, they treat me as the butt of their jokes. I'm their entertainment, their court jester, with my big eyes, my long hair, my big nose, and my melancholy air. That's who my friends are. Do you see those books there and the pile of manuscripts? They are the proof that I lose myself in my work. I passed the Bar examination and I've even argued cases in court. But I quickly realised that my hard work resulted in scoundrels being rewarded and rogues being saved from the scaffold they so richly deserved. I'm ashamed of the profession! I've written...I've written a great deal in order to sooth my poor brain and quench the burning flame. But the remedy hasn't worked. What do you expect? I'm a philosopher and it's as a philosopher I shall die.'

There was a long silence.

'Don't think that I hate humanity for all that,' he continued. 'My goodness no! But I do find men to be useless creatures. I can do without their wit, their writings, and their art. Those meagre brands in the hearth, the murmur of the hot-water bottle, and the purring of the cat have inspired me to write verses a thousand times more beautiful than those of the greatest poets; think thoughts a thousand times more ingenious than those of the greatest philosophers; and express feelings a thousand times more profound than those of the greatest preachers. Why, then, should I read any of their works? Why should I listen to their speeches? And so, for quite a while now, my whole life has been lived in this room and in this armchair, and I think...I think all the time and I never stop. I have here,' he continued, pointing to his forehead, 'I have here treatises on political economics that could revitalise your ruined and degenerate society. I have a philosophical system that can place all human knowledge in a framework and extend it yet further by liberating it from the constraints imposed by professorial teaching. I have plans for houses more comfortable than any you have ever lived in and agricultural projects that could transform France into an immense garden where every citizen could play a productive role. But what's the point of showing what I have done to the world? Will men become any better? Why should I care! Will my pain be relieved? No! Look at the hundreds of manuscripts filling up my attic. They all came out of my head, and I'm still suffering.'

He flung himself down in the armchair again, and continued passionately:

'Do you want to know why the flame inside me burns so brightly and consumes me? It's because I have never cried. Never, no never, has a tear come to moisten my eyelid. See how all around my eyes is black. I'm sure that's the cause: not a single tear has ever fallen to moisten my eyelid. Do you see how pale my lips are and how wrinkled my forehead? That's because the beneficent dew of teardrops has never bathed my grief or relieved my suffering; everything stays inside me, nothing is ever released.'

At this point, his voice faltered:

'Other men, when they suffer, take refuge in the bosom of a friend and return having found consolation. I can't do that. As I told you, I am the Prometheus of this infernal vulture: thought—cruel, incessant, dominating thought. My pain is like a sharp spear that, when I try to throw it away, returns with even greater force against my chest and eats at my heart. Look, I don't know why, but you inspire me with confidence and I'm going to tell you everything. You might as well know: I probably haven't got long to live and I don't want my secrets to die with me. Everything I'm going to tell you is contained there.'

He indicated a pile of dusty papers thrown into a corner of the room. 'But what's all that to you, anyway?'

'No, no, please continue,' I said hastily. 'You've no idea how much you interest me.'

And it was true: I was genuinely moved.

'So, where was I? My God, it's hot in here. It's as if my head is caught in a vice. I really think some ice would do me good. Could you open the window a little?'

I got up in response to his request. When I went over to him, his eyes were closed, his breath was wheezing, and his forehead was bathed in perspiration. He had fallen asleep.

I contemplated him for a long time, this poor sleeper whose sudden effort had used up all his strength, and who lay before me pale, still, and lifeless. The dying embers of the fire illuminated the features of Maximilien Heller who was possessed of a remarkable, almost fantastic, beauty. It was a sad sight to behold, this philosopher who had retired from the company of other men before the age of thirty because he found them "useless"; this dreamer whose dreams had killed him; this thinker whose excesses of thought had made him die of weariness.

The few words I had just exchanged with Maximilien Heller had inspired an indescribable and mysterious sympathy for the unfortunate young man. As I looked at him, I wondered if the invisible cords that tie a being to those of his own kind had been irreparably damaged in his case, and I wondered if there were any way in which I might cure the painful moral illness which consumed him body and soul.

3

I was about to leave, promising myself a return visit shortly to see my interesting patient, when I heard a heavy tread on the stairs and stopped to listen. The steps got closer. Was I imagining things? I even thought I heard the sound of quiet sobbing.

A sudden knock shook the door, and a harsh voice cried:

'Open up in the name of the law!'

The cat jumped out of its skin. Maximilien struggled to open his eyes. His gaze fell on me:

'What? Ah, yes, I remember,' he said in a listless voice. 'But why did you have to wake me by knocking so—?'

A second knock rang out, harder than the first.

'What's this about?' said Maximilien, frowning. 'Please open the door, doctor.'

I obliged.

A fat man wearing a tricolour scarf appeared in the doorway. Several grim-looking individuals stood behind him.

'Excuse me, sir,' said the newcomer, bowing several times. 'I know it's rather late, but duty calls, and I can't put it off till tomorrow. You are Monsieur Maximilien Heller, are you not?'

Maximilien got up and looked calmly at the man in the scarf.

'No, sir' he said, taking a step forward. 'I'm Maximilien Heller.'

'Ah. Terribly sorry, sir. I didn't see you. It's a little dark in here. First off, let me assure you that the sight of my scarf should not trouble you in any way.'

'Sir,' replied the philosopher rather sharply, 'I am not at all well. Please state your business as briefly as possible, so that I may go back to bed.'

The colourful scarf that adorned the fat man's shoulders was deceptive. He was in fact a police inspector performing his duty.

For a moment I was fearful that Maximilien's brusqueness might have rubbed him the wrong way.

Luckily, however, the man was endowed with the qualities of patience, understanding, and politeness that come with years of experience. Accustomed in the course of duty to come up against rude and undisciplined characters, the man had acquired a surprising power. He exuded the calm and the untroubled conscience that justice, like religion, demands of those who would serve it.

'Please be good enough to follow me, sir,' he replied politely. 'We shan't keep you any longer than necessary, but we do need your testimony.'

Maximilien rose painfully from the armchair. He was so weak that I asked the officer whether I might accompany him so he could take my arm.

M. Bienassis—for that was the figure of authority's name—agreed readily.

We walked along the long, dark, corridor and reached a door that was scarcely visible in the darkness.

One of the other officers raised his lamp and a workman that had also been brought along smashed the lock with a quick hammer blow.

A gust of icy wind blew in our faces.

'Huh!' growled yet another officer behind me. 'He could at least have shut the window before he left.'

'Gustave' said M. Bienassis, turning to another of the men behind him. 'Light a candle and shut that window.'

The man did as he was told. We entered an attic room even smaller than Maximilien's. The only furniture was a table, two chairs, and a bed on which lay a disgusting straw mattress.

In one corner of the room we could make out a small chest with a padlock.

The inspector sat down at the table and spread out several papers taken from a large wallet. After beckoning Maximilien to sit down next to him, he made a sign to one of his men who went to the door and shouted:

'Bring in the accused.'

I stood behind M. Heller.

There was the sound of steps in the corridor and then a pale wild-eyed man with frizzled hair appeared in the attic doorway, supported by two police officers.

'Come over here!' ordered M. Bienassis, watching the new arrival attentively over gold-rimmed spectacles.

With the help of the two officers, the man took several steps into the room.

'Is your name Jean-Louis Guérin?' asked M. Bienassis.

The unfortunate man stared vacantly at the inspector without answering.

'Have you been, for the last week, in the employ of M. Bréhat-Lenoir?'

No answer. The inspector continued calmly:

'Are you aware of the accusations against you? You are suspected of having poisoned your master. What do you have to say?'

The accused started to shake convulsively. He opened his mouth several times to speak but was paralysed by fear, and the sounds coming out of his throat were unintelligible.

'Look here, Guérin,' the inspector continued, looking away from the accused and pretending to sort through the papers in front of him. 'We're not judges or executioners and we've no desire to hurt you. You can speak without fear here. You can say anything you like, but you must speak. It may well be that you are innocent, even though the charges against you are very serious. I have to warn you that your silence and discomfort could be misinterpreted and used against you. Do you admit to having purchased arsenic the day before yesterday from Legras the herbalist?'

The accused made a violent effort to free himself from the officers holding him, but in vain; he saw that his struggles were useless and that escape was impossible. Tears started to stream from his eyes and he said, in a voice broken by sobs:

'Let me go! Let me go! I'm innocent. I'm an honest man, I swear it. Ask the people; ask the people where I come from. They'll tell you I'm an honest man. I've a poor old mother. I came to Paris to earn some money because she's sick and can't work. Me a murderer? Oh, my God! My God!'

He tried to hold his manacled hands up to the heavens, but suddenly all his force left him and if the officers hadn't held him firmly, he would have fallen face down on the attic floor.

'Put him on the bed,' said Bienassis, indicating the straw mattress in the corner of the little room.

Maximilien placed his long, slender hand on the inspector's shoulder.

'Are you saying, sir, that this man is a murderer?'

M. Bienassis turned round, somewhat surprised, and shook his head.

'The charges against him are damning,' he murmured in a voice so low that only we could hear. 'But I have to agree he doesn't look like a criminal. We can't have it both ways: either this man is perfectly innocent or he's a dastardly villain and a remarkable actor.'

M. Bienassis made another sign to one of the officers to keep an eye on Guérin in case the fainting had been feigned. Turning to the locksmith, who was standing next to him awaiting orders, he said:

'Open the chest and let's get a move on.'

With a couple of hammer blows the locksmith smashed the padlock on the black chest. The inspector, candle in hand, went over and lifted the lid.

The chest was full of rough peasant outer garments and underwear, but the garments had been carefully brushed, and the underwear, scrupulously white, bore the rustic aroma of lavender. All the humble objects were arranged with a care that bore witness to a woman's hand: that of an attentive and thoughtful mother.

The unfortunate Guérin had by now recovered from his fainting fit and had been seated on a chair. With tear-filled eyes, he followed the actions of the officers who rapidly destroyed the painstaking arrangement, unfolding the poor fellow's clothes, shaking them, searching the pockets, and feeling the lining.

'Here! A noose made of ribbons,' one of the officers said suddenly, pulling a faded bouquet wrapped in pink ribbons out of the chest.

He threw it jokingly to one of his colleagues.

'Take it, Gustave,' he said. 'You can give it to the accused.'

M. Bienassis looked angrily at the officer. On hearing the cruel joke, the accused had shot out of his chair and clasped his manacled hands together with all his force.

Maximilien Heller had also stood up and was looking about him with a doleful air.

'Inspector, sir,' said the accused in an imploring voice, 'would you let me have that garland of ribbons?'

'Show me that,' said M. Bienassis.

He examined the bunch of ribbons for several minutes, patted it all over, seemed to hesitate for a second, then ordered it to be handed over to the accused.

Meanwhile, the officers continued their search under the attentive eye of the inspector; but even though they went through the clothes over and over again and poked into every corner of the chest, they apparently did not find what they were looking for.

'Stop searching the chest,' said M. Bienassis, after it became obvious that the search had been fruitless. 'Turn your attention to the straw mattress. We may find the money there.'

The mattress was subjected to the same treatment, with the same result.

The inspector didn't give up, however; he made his officers inspect, with the utmost care, the tiles of the floor; he made them break apart the wood of the chairs in case they had been hollowed out to hide gold; the table was demolished; the walls were tapped with a hammer; even the ashes in the hearth were raked through with great care.

Eventually, after more than an hour of meticulous work, the officers stopped, exhausted, looking as sheepishly at each other as hunters who have beaten the bushes for a day without finding any game.

'It's incomprehensible. It's truly unbelievable,' murmured M. Bienassis, as he sat holding his head in both hands. 'What happened to the money? The man had no contacts in Paris and obviously no accomplices. The crime was committed yesterday, we arrested him an hour ago, and yet it's impossible to lay our hands on the loot.'

The philosopher appeared not to be paying any attention to the policeman's monologue; his attention seemed fixed on Guérin, whose bewildered facial expression he was studying with interest.

After a few minutes of reflection, M. Bienassis apparently decided on a new line of approach with the accused.

'The results of our search seem to bear out your claim,' he told him. 'Don't think for a moment, however, that the police will give up their investigation. A considerable sum of money was stolen on the night of the murder; it must be found, and it will be. You remain under the gravest suspicion; everything points to you as M. Bréhat-Lenoir's killer: we have tangible proof to that effect. There's only one way you can save yourself: the truth. Admit the crime, tell us where the money is hidden, and reveal the names of your accomplices; justice will take account of your sincerity and you will be spared the capital punishment which now threatens your life.'

The accused murmured his reply in a voice broken with emotion:

'I'm innocent.'

'Think again: tomorrow may be too late. Justice will have discovered what you have been hiding and there won't be any more confessions to make.'

'I'm innocent.'

'Fine. From now on it won't be me that deals with you. The examining magistrate will know what he has to do.'

The inspector turned to Maximilien Heller.

'I'm sorry that you had to witness that scene, sir, but your testimony may well prove important to us and I ask you to tell us all you know about the accused. He spent a week in a room close to yours before finding a place. Did you notice anything suspicious in his behaviour during that time?'

'So that's why you brought me here?'

'Quite; one doesn't spend time next to a man without learning something of his habits and the company he keeps. Did he have any visitors in the short time he was here? Did you ever hear the sound of a voice? Did he go out often, day or night?'

The philosopher stood up and went over to Guérin, whom he observed for a moment with his calm, steady eye.

'You were supposed to marry, weren't you, upon your return home?'

'Yes, sir,' replied the accused, rolling his eyes in alarm.

'Well, you can order your wedding clothes; and you,' he said, addressing the police officers who were watching him with their mouths open, 'watch over him carefully because in two months he will be free.'

So saying, Maximilien Heller wrapped himself in his greatcoat and left the room with the haughty air of a Don Quixote defying his windmills.

I turned to the inspector, who was muttering to himself while gathering his papers:

'This is strange. This is all very strange.'

'Please excuse my friend, my dear sir,' I said with some embarrassment. 'He's not well, you understand——.'

'Your friend, sir, can explain himself before the judge,' replied the inspector, with a note of bitterness in his voice. 'As for me, my job here is finished and it only remains for me to submit my report.'

And with these words he left, accompanied by a squad of agents surrounding the accused. The sound of their steps on the stairs gradually faded away and everything fell silent.

I hastened to rejoin Maximilien Heller.

I found him sitting in his armchair, attempting to poke the dying fire with a pair of tongs.

'Well, what did you think of all that?'

He shrugged his shoulders.

'I shall probably be a famous martyr,' he replied calmly.

'Do you think that man is innocent?'

'Yes, I do. But, after all, what does it matter?'

He leant back in his armchair and closed his eyes. Despite the seeming indifference, it was plain to see he was in the grip of a strong emotion. His hands, in a state of constant agitation, slid feverishly to and fro along the armrests.

His mind was obviously racing and his fertile imagination was full of the sad spectacle he had just witnessed.

'Do you realise,' I said with a smile, 'that your comportment has no doubt planted a few suspicions in the worthy inspector's mind. By refusing to testify, do you not fear being classified as an accomplice? In other times, that would have been enough to get you hanged.'

'Yes, but you also know that in other times a rather too celebrated policeman would have condemned a man to death based purely on the lines of his hand. Maybe now you understand my silence.'

At that moment the Saint-Roch clock struck midnight.

'You're tired,' I said to Maximilien. 'I'm going to let you sleep.'

'In fact, this evening I feel more tired than usual; I shall throw myself on the bed and take a dash of opium to help me get some much-needed sleep.'

As I was leaving, he said to me, with great insistence:

'Come early tomorrow, I'll be waiting for you. We need to talk. You will come, won't you?'

'I promise.'

I shook his hand and left, still badly shaken by what I had seen in the course of the evening.

As I came out of the house, I bought an evening paper and read the following in the 'news in brief':

A mysterious incident has caused consternation in the Luxembourg quarter. M. Bréhat-Lenoir, the famous banker who had retired from the world of finance a few years ago after amassing a vast fortune, was found dead in his bed two days ago. At first an attack of apoplexy was suspected: M. Bréhat-Lenoir was excessively overweight and led a sedentary life. Later, however, foul play was suspected. M. Castille, the deceased's nephew, noticed that the banker's writing desk had been forced open and a number of papers scattered. A glass on a nearby table was taken away for analysis and arsenic was discovered in the drops of liqueur it contained. The deceased did not leave a will, so his immense fortune will go to his brother M. Bréhat-Kerguen.

A little further on, there was the following:

As we were going to press, we learned that the police have discovered the identity of M. Bréhat-Lenoir's killer. It is said to be a servant named Guérin, who has been in the deceased's service for only a week. Motivated simply by greed, the wretch poisoned his master. He claimed that rats infested his bedroom and he bought a small amount of arsenic, which he mixed into the beverage M. Bréhat-Lenoir was in the habit of drinking every night. The servant's story was so crude that, in spite of his protests of innocence and his laughable attempt at fainting, he was placed under arrest. At present, he is in the hands of the police. An affair that at first appeared to have some intriguing details and a possibly tortuous plot was thus reduced to a banal case of theft.

The next day, around ten o'clock, I received a visit from my tutor, Doctor B…; he seemed anxious and preoccupied.

'Have you heard about this Bréhat-Lenoir business?' he asked me after a few moments of idle chat, looking at me over his spectacles.

I showed him the newspaper I had bought the night before.

'All I know is what's in this article,' I replied.

'Ah, but don't you realise it's very serious, and above all, very mysterious? I was called in yesterday evening to do the autopsy. Would you believe that, after a long and exhaustive examination, I couldn't find the slightest trace of arsenic?'

'That's going to play havoc with the investigation.'

'I think the police were surprised, to say the least, and not at all happy to see their theories overturned right at the outset. But they're not giving up. I got a letter this morning from the examining magistrate to whom I'd sent my report yesterday evening. He asked me to present it at the inquest today.'

'Why? For what purpose?'

'I don't know. But here's what's curious: do you know who they've invited as well?'

'Who?'

'Doctor Wickson.'

'What? The scheming fellow who made such a fuss about finely-ground powder ten years ago?'

'The very same.'

'The one you so fiercely opposed in the name of science?'

'Yes. The Academy backed me up, but public opinion was against me and was much taken with Indian medicine. So, the man is here in Paris. What a coincidence. I don't know what it's all about: I thought the fellow was dead and buried years ago. His ideas are more in vogue than ever, and justice, as you know, doesn't shy away from popular science. If the judge had his wits about him, he wouldn't have put me in the position of debating with someone I had so vigorously opposed in the past. You understand, I trust, that it's out of the question for me to go and I'm counting on you to replace me. I know you've made a very thorough study of poisons and you know every bit as much as I do on the subject.'

I nodded my head in acknowledgment of the not entirely disinterested flattery from the great man.

'So, it's agreed, then. You should be at 102, Rue Cassette at one o'clock. That's the deceased's residence. Here's a letter to the examining magistrate giving a pretext for my absence. You should give it to him.'

Whereupon Dr. B… rose and shook my hand with a certain degree of emotion:

'On your way, dear boy,' he said. 'Try and convince the magistrate, and above all, don't let Wickson get under your skin. Remember our professional honour is in your hands: defend it against ignorance and charlatanism. Don't forget to let me know how it went, the minute the inquest is over.'

Dr. B…'s voice trembled a little as he spoke those words. The gleam in his eye betrayed the intense interest my aged professor had in the outcome of the impending fight. Wickson was the only person in the world that the good doctor truly hated.

I promised him that I would do my very best to uphold the principles of true science and to ensure his opinion prevailed.

An hour later, I was in Maximilien Heller's attic.

The philosopher appeared calmer than the night before; his fever had almost entirely abated.

'I feel much better this morning,' he told me. 'Your company yesterday was a great relief to me. There are times, rare enough, when solitude is bad for me. And yesterday I was haunted by the memory of a terrible anniversary. But let that pass. Have you any more details about the mysterious events? I've been thinking about it all night. It's obvious the man is innocent.'

I handed him the paper from the night before, which he read very carefully, then murmured:

'I'd be really interested to see how this turns out.'

'If you wish, I can get you into the house where the crime took place and you can be present at the autopsy.'

'Really?' he said, viewing me with surprise. 'And how, may I ask, can that be?'

I told him about my brief discussion with Dr. B…, and the part I had agreed to play.

'Well, I'll certainly come with you,' said Maximilien Heller in a resolute tone. 'I need to know what it all means. This will be the first time in two years that I set foot outside this room. I sense I am entering a new life. What would you say if I were to save this man from the scaffold? Wouldn't that be strange? I would become a philanthropist. But it's not for love of mankind that I'm doing this; on the contrary, it's to show up all the vice in the system. For, without me, if everything followed its natural course, an innocent man would die, condemned by the sentence of his fellow men.'

I couldn't suppress a smile.

'Are you so sure that Guérin is not guilty?'

'Yes.'

'Are you convinced you can prove his innocence?'

'Yes.'

'And can you find the real guilty party?'

'Yes.'

He paced up and down the attic with his long stride, like a lion impatient to be free of his cage.

'Yes!' he cried elatedly. 'I want to see the daylight again. Yes! I return today to the world I left voluntarily. There's a mystery there that I want to solve, shadows that I want to sweep aside. I've resolved the most challenging social problems: why not this one in the same way? On the day they erect the scaffold for this unfortunate man, I want to appear before them dragging the real culprit behind me, throw him at the executioner's feet, and take back this innocent. But don't think I'm interested in the man himself. Why should I care whether he lives or not?'

Maximilien was transfigured. His face, pale and hollow from long suffering, was suffused with an almost supernatural glow; his posture, made languid by fever, had regained all its natural vigour. His gestures were firm and determined and his handsome head was held high.

I still recall, after so many years, the remarkable effect that Maximilien Heller's voice and attitude had on me at the time. I felt a sort of uneasy surprise. I feared, I admit, that the grandiloquence and the prophetic tone were merely early signs of a mental breakdown whose symptoms I thought I might have detected previously in M. Heller. I took hold of his hand: it was cold; his pulse was normal. I looked him in the eye and was struck by his calm and resolute expression. Words cannot describe the sense of happiness and gratitude to Providence that flooded over me. The truth dawned on me: I had read it in Maximilien's clear and limpid regard. I smiled as I thought of the bitterness with which he had felt obliged to imbue his words. The would-be philosopher had tried in vain to hide his true sentiments. It was not an implacable hatred of society and its laws that inspired such a generous resolve. God had just placed in his path a victim in need of consoling, an innocent to be saved from the executioner, and Maximilien's heart had melted with pity in the face of the poor unfortunate, on whom man's justice was about to bear down. By virtue of this noble intent, his life had been given a direction and a goal. A strong and mysterious bond now reunited him with the world from which he had so abruptly separated himself, in a single moment of pride, or perhaps anguish.

I let go of the hand I had briefly held in mine.

"God be praised," I thought. "Maximilien will live."

M. Heller opened a small wardrobe and brought out a long brown frock coat and a rather old-fashioned hat. The philosopher seemed to have no pretensions to elegance.

'It'll soon be noon,' he observed, as if to explain his obvious impatience. 'Maybe we should be on our way.'

'Very well,' I replied. 'We'll have plenty of time to examine the scene of the crime.'

'That's very important,' murmured the philosopher, opening the door for me.

We hailed a cab. Half an hour later we pulled up outside 102, Rue Cassette.

I rang the doorbell, and soon the heavy *porte-cochère* swung open with a groan. We entered a damp courtyard, so overgrown with grass it could have served as a pasture.

At the rear rose a large four-storey building whose windows were all shuttered. With five or six long strides, we reached an oak door with a peephole. A thick iron wire stretched across the courtyard and served to open the *porte-cochère* without the need for anyone to leave the building, which resembled a gloomy fortress.

Maximilien lifted and let fall the heavy iron knocker, sending shudders through the long corridors. A narrow window opened suddenly, the door swung ajar, and we could see a thin, frail, old man in short trousers who stared wide-eyed at the bizarre clothes and even more bizarre countenance of the philosopher.

'Monsieur,' I explained, to calm his nerves, 'Doctor B… could not be present at the inquest and has sent me in his stead.'

'Very well, monsieur,' replied the little man, opening the door to let us past. 'Forgive me, but we have been so shocked by the dreadful accident. Poor M. Bréhat-Lenoir, such a good master. He was so afraid of being murdered that he barricaded himself in his bedroom. It's awful, isn't it? Please be good enough to wait here; when the magistrate arrives, I'll come and get you.'

He led us into a large room hung with old tapestries whose patterns had almost completely faded away. Four windows looked onto a dark, sad garden planted with large trees and surrounded by ivy-covered walls.

The philosopher advanced towards the windows and pressed his pale forehead against one of them.

We remained like that for about ten minutes, I watching him in silence while walking up and down the room, he peering out of the window, his body bursting with nervous impatience.

The sound of a heavy, uneven tread resonated in the corridor. Maximilien raised his head expectantly; the slightest noise seemed to affect him. The door to the garden opened, there was a crunching noise on the sand, and a heavily-built white-haired man with a stoop passed rapidly in front of the windows.

At the sight of the man, the philosopher looked startled and shrank back as if he had stood on a snake.

'What's the matter?' I asked, surprised at his strange reaction.

'It's nothing... nothing,' he replied in a subdued voice. 'Just a dizzy spell, I think.'

He took up his position by the window again and watched the stranger who, after having taken a diagonal path across the garden, left through a door hidden behind the ivy. We waited a few more minutes.

Soon the pale figure of the little manservant, M. Prosper, appeared in the doorway.

'Did the gentlemen call?' he asked timidly.

The good fellow was obviously eager to engage us in conversation and I, in turn, wished to pose him a number of questions.

'It's very hot in here,' I said to him. 'Couldn't you open this window?'

He climbed on to a chair with the agility of a squirrel and did what I asked.

'It's one o'clock,' he announced, with a sideways glance at the large copper clock situated on the mantelpiece. 'The other gentlemen are late.'

'Tell me frankly, steward,' I said looking him straight in the eye. 'Do you believe the man arrested yesterday is the guilty party?'

The little old man's eyebrows shot up and his grey eyes widened. Taking a pinch of snuff with all the majesty of a marquis of the old school, he replied in his squeaky voice:

'Monsieur, it's a very serious matter to accuse a man when one isn't in possession of concrete proof. All I can say is that there is some very serious circumstantial evidence against him. I can still hear him saying to me, in his patois: "They be rats in me room…best I go t'the bonesetter."'

'Did he really say that?' asked Maximilien, sharply.

'As surely as I'm standing here.'

'That's really curious.'

So saying, the philosopher returned to his thoughts.

'But what's all this I hear about a will?' I continued.

A malicious expression flitted across the little manservant's weasel face.

'Here's the gist of it,' he replied. 'You know that my master was, shall we say, of an original turn of mind. For forty years he had been at loggerheads with his brother, M. Bréhat-Kerguen, another bizarre character who almost never left his hole in Brittany, and whom we saw for the first time this morning.'

'Ah. Is he here?'

'He just walked in front of the windows a few minutes ago: you must have seen him.'

The philosopher murmured something unintelligible.

'Yes,' continued the manservant, 'he arrived this morning. 'Who alerted him? I don't know. He's like a wild beast and only addressed a few words to me to the effect that he wouldn't be attending the autopsy because it would be too painful, etc. etc., before leaving.'

'So there's an exit door in the garden?'

'Yes, it gives on to Rue Vaugirard, near the Hôtel du Renard Bleu. So, to finish up the story, everyone thought that, given the bad blood between the brothers, my master would disinherit him. Judge for yourself: a man who looks more like a wolf than a human being; a man who married his servant. M. Castille, M. Bréhat-Lenoir's nephew, assumed he was the heir. But would you believe that, even though they brought in a justice of the peace to go through all the master's papers, and even open his writing desk, they couldn't find the slightest trace of a last will and testament? Which means that all my master's millions will go to that crazy old man Bréhat-Kerguen. As for me, who served him devotedly for twenty years and who only managed to save a meagre amount—.'

Maximilien interrupted him:

'Did they seal your master's room?'

'Of course. And I was appointed guardian, which gave me some cause for concern because of the responsibility involved. You should have heard the curses coming out of that brute Bréhat-Kerguen's mouth this morning when he discovered the seals on his brother's room.'

'Really!' said Maximilien.

'My god, the language! And he locked himself in his room to calm down, grumbling all the while.'

We heard the rumbling of a carriage pulling up to the *porte-cochère*.

'Here's the magistrate,' announced the manservant.

Maximilien made a sign to me that I readily understood.

'Steward,' I said to the little man, who was obviously flattered by the title, 'could you tell us in which room the inquest will be held.'

'Up the stairs, on the right, at the end of the corridor,' he replied quickly.

And, on hearing the sound of the doorbell sending reverberations through the ancient walls, he rushed to the door.

We climbed the great wooden staircase and entered a chamber whose windows overlooked the garden,

The body, covered by a sheet, was laid out on a table made of white wood.

At the rear of the chamber, covered with seals, was the communicating door to the deceased's bedroom.

Maximilien Heller ducked behind one of the long window curtains; that way he could see everything without being seen. At that very moment, the door of the chamber opened and the crown prosecutor and the examining magistrate appeared, the latter with his clerk.

The little manservant led them into the chamber with a pleasant smile which turned into a scowl of astonishment when he saw that I was alone in the room.

The crown prosecutor having, with majestic dignity, made an imperious sign for him to leave, he had no choice but to do so, sparing me the awkward explanation for the disappearance of Maximilien.

I introduced myself to the gentlemen and handed over the letter from Dr. B… in which he excused himself from the proceedings.

'Good grief!' exclaimed the examining magistrate, taking a rapid pinch of snuff, 'I'd completely forgotten that Dr. Wickson was not exactly in Dr. B…'s good books. What do you expect? It's such a long time ago, and I've so many things on my mind. Please offer my apologies to your tutor, although I don't regret the error all that much, since it has allowed me the pleasure of making your acquaintance.'

And he smiled pleasantly as he spoke.

As for the crown prosecutor—an important personage with a pale, austere face framed by black sideburns, aristocratic hands, and an icy composure—he continued examining Dr. B...'s report of the day before.

The body lay open in conformance with the regulations, the intestines and the internal organs having been placed in separate jars.

'I haven't eaten, dammit!' exclaimed the examining magistrate in a resounding voice. 'It's about time Dr. Wickson got here. We're here at his request and I find it very peculiar that he keeps us waiting. What's more—.'

The sound of the doorbell interrupted the dignified figure.

'Here he is,' he continued, lowering his voice.

The crown prosecutor drew himself up to his full height and the examining magistrate adjusted his collar. As for me, I felt like a conscript going into the line of fire. To boost my morale, I thought of my old tutor who had placed his full confidence in me, and who would be waiting impatiently for the outcome of the inquest.

Silence reigned in the chamber. Not a word was exchanged between us until M. Prosper, opening the door, announced in his squeaky voice:

'Doctor Wickson.'

A man of about fifty, with a Herculean build, a ruddy complexion, and striking blond hair came towards us and said, with a slight British accent:

'A thousand pardons, gentlemen, for having made you wait for an appointment I myself requested. But, just as I was leaving my house, I received a call to help a dying man.'

'And you saved him, no doubt?' asked the examining magistrate, sympathetically.

'Of course,' replied the Englishman, imperturbably. 'I saved him.'

He looked around as he spoke and appeared surprised not to see Dr. B....

'But,' he continued, 'I don't see the distinguished doctor who was going to do me the honour of discussing my medical opinion?'

I repeated the pretext that Dr. B.... had asked me to use concerning his absence. He smiled imperceptibly.

'Please convey to Dr. B.... my excuses for my presumptuousness in challenging the experiments he has conducted with such care and scientific precision. However, I have carried out profound studies in the matter of poisons, in particular the arsenic-based ones, which is why I have proposed a second inquest. My greatest desire, believe me, is to find that my conclusions conform to those of your deeply respected tutor.'

I bowed coldly and proposed that the examination begin without further ado; the crestfallen features of the hungry examining magistrate filled me with a sincere pity.

The two magistrates took up their places at the feet of the corpse, towards the door; Dr. Wickson and I, to the left, faced the window.

Much as I would like to spare my readers the description of the autopsy, I must enter into such detail as is indispensable to the understanding of the story.

The task of the medical examiner has been facilitated for several years now, thanks to the invention of the English chemist James Marsh, who discovered an ingenious method of discovering even the faintest traces of arsenic in the body.

Here, in a few words, is a description of the apparatus used:

It's a simple glass flask filled with hydrogen, into which is placed the substance to be examined. The arsenic combines with the hydrogen gas and the combination escapes through the slender orifice of the flask. The jet of gas is then lit and a white porcelain saucer held against it. If the slightest trace of arsenic is present, black streaks are deposited on the porcelain.

Dr. Wickson produced such a flask from the folds of his greatcoat. But I noticed that the glass wasn't very clear, and I asked him to use the one I had brought along. He examined it meticulously for a long time and eventually accepted it, while concealing his annoyance.

I approached the jars containing the internal organs in order to remove the lids, but the Englishman prevented me and pulled the sealed covers off impatiently.

I noticed that he kept his white gloves while he was doing it.

'Gentlemen,' he said in a solemn voice, addressing the magistrates but without looking at them, you are doubtless aware of the workings of this apparatus. I shall direct a jet of gas against these panes of glass. If there is any arsenic in the portion of the organs that I have placed in the flask the pane will immediately blacken.

I thought he sounded like a charlatan reciting his patter.

He went towards the window adjacent to the one where the philosopher was hiding, and directed the gas flame on to the pane.

We couldn't help our expressions of surprise. The glass was suddenly covered with black streaks. At the same time, a strong smell of garlic pervaded the chamber, signalling the presence of toxic matter.

My poor professor had been defeated in the first round. The examining magistrate shot me a politely ironic look:

'Oh, oh!' he said. 'That doesn't look good for you,'

'I will only regard the experiment as conclusive' I said, 'if I am allowed to conduct the same experiments myself.'

The Englishman, despite his success, remained impassive, and he handed me his flask graciously.

I performed the experiment: the window pane blackened again with an intensity that proved an abundance of the toxic matter. I repeated it three or four time, always with the same result.

The curtain that Maximilien Heller was standing behind moved slightly. I became anxious, for it seemed to me that the Englishman had caught the movement out of the corner of his eye.

It turned out to be nothing, for he resumed his natural smile and turned to the magistrates:

'It would seem that the experiment has been decisive,' he said. 'And please note that I used the apparatus provided by Dr. B....'

'I have no objection,' I replied, in truth vexed by such sudden and unexpected results.

'So, then Monsieur,' said the public prosecutor, speaking for the first time, 'are you willing to sign the minutes and the report that confirms the presence of poison in the deceased's body?'

I nodded in assent.

'Clerk,' continued the haughty magistrate, turning towards an insignificant little man scribbling away in a corner of the room. 'Please bring the report and the minutes for the gentlemen to sign.'

Dr. Wickson signed—without removing his gloves—and I signed in turn.

The Englishman appeared to be having some difficulty containing his glee.

He took his leave gravely and I followed with rather a bad grace. Just before he left, Wickson once again asked me to convey his deepest respects to Dr. B....

'Monsieur de Ribeyrac,' said the examining magistrate as he was leaving, 'you will be lunching with me, I trust? I'm dying of hunger.'

That day, the students of Dr. B...'s class didn't know what to make of his distracted manner, his nervous gestures and the general bad mood of their elderly professor.

8

I took a few steps towards the door, following the good gentlemen, and bade them farewell once more.

M. Prosper escorted them to the door, then turned towards me with a secretive air; he was obviously itching to know what happened but I felt under no obligation to inform him.

'There are a few matters I have to attend to,' I said, going back up the stairs. 'Please leave me alone for another half hour with the corpse.'

'Why, monsieur, stay as long as you wish,' replied the little manservant, in honeyed tones. As for me, I shall go up to M. Bréhat-Kerguen's room to see if he needs anything. He's double-locked his door, the cunning devil, and made me swear I don't have a duplicate key. Well, I swore, heh, heh!' he continued, pulling a huge set of keys from his pocket. 'But I still need to take a look inside his room: M. Castille strongly advised me not to let his inheritance deteriorate.'

Just at the moment I opened the door of the chamber, the old fellow—whose dominant fault was clearly an overwhelming curiosity—managed to sneak a glance into the room to assure himself that Maximilien Heller was still there, then shook his head as if to tell himself it was just a whim, and continued up to the second floor.

The philosopher had come out of hiding and was carefully examining the jars and the flask that had been used during the autopsy.

He looked up and said, with a wry smile:

'So! You didn't have much luck, doctor, and there certainly seems to have been poison used, but, for Heaven's sake, why didn't you make him take off his gloves?'

I stared at him, taken aback by his question.

'Come over here,' he said, indicating the edge of the table.

'What is it?'

'Look more closely. Don't you see anything?'

I noticed a few traces of a fine white powder on the wood.

'Arsenic!' I exclaimed, dumbfounded.

'Exactly,' replied Maximilien. 'Now, how do you explain the presence of arsenic on the table? You didn't put it there, did you? So it was your adversary.'

'That's quite an allegation.'

'Did you notice that he kept his gloves on throughout the operation?'

'Yes.'

'Did you notice that he frequently, almost absent-mindedly, placed his right hand exactly where you now see the white powder? And that, once, he placed his hand to his lips and pulled it away hastily as if repulsed?'

'No.'

'That's right, you didn't have my angle of view. But I noticed a few other strange things: for example, why did he want to remove the jar covers himself? Why did he cut the internal organs himself with scissors from his own trouser pockets? Your trust in his good faith does you honour, doctor, but, in my opinion it was misplaced.'

'So, you believe——.'

'I believe, or rather I am convinced, that the magistrates and you fell into a trap. That man put arsenic in his gloves, one finger of which was pierced, and he poisoned everything he touched.'

'I don't see what benefit he gained by tricking us like that.'

'Benefit, benefit... you're talking like a lawyer,' exclaimed my strange friend, shrugging his shoulders. 'What do I care about that? I'm not even going to try to guess, because it's down that tricky path that justice always loses its way. I'm only interested in the facts. When I have them all in my hands, amongst all the improbabilities that appear so strange at first, you will see the truth shine, more brilliantly than the sun.'

He drew himself up to his full height, his eyes gleaming like diamonds.

'The truth,' he exclaimed, indicating vigorously the door covered with seals, 'is in that room. And the day I manage to get inside, I shall discover it.'

Then, jamming his hat down over his eyes, he left and I heard him descend the stairs rapidly.

I followed him.

At the foot of the stairs, I found him in conversation with M. Prosper. He muttered a few words in a low voice then took me by the arm with one of his customary abrupt gestures, and made towards the door.

I offered him a cigar and flicked the lighter but the tinder wouldn't light because of the damp weather.

'Wait!' cried the helpful little manservant, fumbling in his pockets. 'Take this.'

He handed me a piece of paper which I lit and offered to Maximilien.

He brought it to his lips to light the tobacco, but suddenly his eyes widened and he quickly blew out the flame, stuffed the paper in his pocket, and ran away with such alacrity that M. Prosper was moved to say:

'That poor young man. He's completely lost his head.'

9

I lost sight of M. Maximilien Heller for a couple of weeks. Caught up in work and in the whirl of those matters, serious and frivolous, that make up life, I had started to forget about the case when, one bright morning around eight o'clock, my manservant informed me that someone desired to speak with me immediately.

I gave the order to admit him.

A tall young man came into the room. With his dyed blond hair, his wide-open eyes and the placid expression on his beaming features, he epitomised the kind of empty-headed fop so popular in the theatre at the time.

He greeted me no less than three times, then stood there in front of me twirling his hat in his fingers.

'Monthieur,' he started, with a pronounced lisp, 'I'm theeking employment. I come to athk whether monthieur hath need of a thervant.'

'And who exactly recommended you? Have you a letter?'

I got no further because the peasant with the inane expression suddenly raised the blond wig that had almost covered his eyes, to reveal the black locks and high forehead of my friend Maximilien Heller.

'What! Is that you?' I asked in astonishment. 'Why are you in disguise? Are the police after you?'

'Aha!' he responded, with silent mirth. 'You thought I was becoming more and more unhinged, didn't you? And right at this moment you wouldn't think twice about sending me to the madhouse to join my peers. I'll explain my behaviour which, I do understand, must appear bizarre to you. The person you saw before you just now is in service — no, don't look so surprised. Under the skin of the buffoon is the skin of the fox I'm obliged to hide. And guess who my employer is: none other than M. Bréhat-Kerguen.'

The incoherent babble of words and his bizarre appearance did indeed cause me to believe for a brief moment that he really was mad. He continued:

'Don't be so scared and listen to me. You know I trust you. I'm going to tell you all I've found out. But you must swear to me that you'll keep it to yourself. In any case, the only reason I'm telling you is because I'm going to need your help for what comes next; otherwise nobody in the world would know the extraordinary things I've discovered.'

I made the promise. He went to the door, locked it, then came over to sit close to the hearth. After a few moments of silence, as if he were trying to gather his thoughts, he started to talk:

'You no doubt remember that the last time I saw you—the day of the autopsy—I told you that the method by which I hoped to solve this bloody mystery would be totally different from that usually followed by the police.

'They try to determine the criminal's motive and thus pit the unknown against the known. The process is inherently defective: the arrest of Guérin is the proof. My approach is to go from the known to the unknown. I follow the facts and nothing but the facts—without worrying about motive or the identity of the assailant. I assemble them, no matter how contradictory they may appear to be, and at some point, the light shines.

'It so happens that I now have the facts, apart from a few minor ones I hope to have shortly. And I must say that luck—that grand master—has served me well. Do you remember you tried to light your cigar as we were leaving the banker's house and the dampness prevented the lighter from working? M. Prosper, the eager steward, offered you a piece of paper he took from his pocket? '

'Very well.'

'Then you offered me the burning paper and just as I brought it to my lips, I appeared startled and departed suddenly, leaving you no doubt dumbfounded about my bizarre behaviour?'

'Too true.'

He took out of his jacket pocket a partially burnt piece of paper and handed it to me. As I turned it around in my fingers, the philosopher, smiling, asked:

'You don't see anything remarkable, do you? Well, you'll be surprised to learn that this scrap of paper is, to a large extent, the key to the puzzle. Take these tweezers and hold it over the embers in the hearth. If you look carefully, you'll realise why I was so excited the other day.'

I did as he asked. When heated, the paper twisted itself in a spiral. I unwound it and saw a number of signs clearly drawn in blue ink.

'I have to say,' I told the philosopher, shaking my head, 'that I'm no wiser than before. I await your explanation of the riddle.'

'It's quite a story,' replied Maximilien Heller, leaning back in his armchair. And I admit that I'd have looked a long time for the solution, just like you, and might never have found it but for an extraordinary stroke of luck.

'I told you that I had once been a lawyer and had argued several cases.

'It was in 1832. I was in training full of the crusading zeal that consumes young professionals at the start of their career.

'One of my first cases was that of a certain Jules Lanseigne, involved in a mysterious business that the police had never really managed to fully penetrate. There was a group of gangsters who had terrorised Paris through a number of incredibly audacious thefts. They were so skilful that it was only after many years, and thanks to the genius of a celebrated police detective, that they were eventually caught.

'Even so, not all of them were apprehended. Only three were brought to trial. They were Jacques Pichet, Paul Robert, and Jules Lanseigne, known as *Little Dagger*.

'The master mind who ran the operation so effectively escaped arrest and those captured stubbornly refused to reveal his name. All anyone knew was that, inside the gang, he was known by the curious nickname of Red Bomber.

'One of the men was in possession of letters written in almost indecipherable hieroglyphics, only a few of which were decoded by the illustrious detective who had made the arrests.

'The first of the accused was condemned to death, the second to twenty years of hard labour, and my client—against whom the case was weakest—to five years of prison.

'I found the trial fascinating, and I had the opportunity of frequent meetings with the celebrated detective. He recounted, in great detail, all the events and excursions of the fight he had waged against the gang for four years: a fight that had resulted in three of them being brought to justice.

'Alas! The poor fellow died without the consolation of arresting the leader, and I believe that failure hastened his demise. He had explained to me, with an impressive lucidity, the hieroglyphic signs found on the criminals; and it's because of those lessons and what I remembered that I was able to decipher the puzzle.

'I'll explain as briefly as possible:

'The first thing to notice is that we only have a fragment of a letter, a postscript, the main body of the letter having unfortunately been destroyed by fire.

'Look at the signature: the sign with the "r" inside means Red Bomber. It's the seal of the master criminal who proved himself more adroit than the entire police force.

'The envelope sign means: *write*

'The pierced heart is the sign of *Little Dagger* (the name adopted by my old client Jules Lanseigne.)

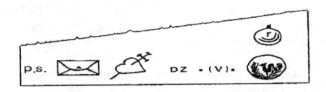

'"DZ." The gang changed letters into numbers and numbers into letters, so D, the fourth letter of the alphabet, stands for 4 and Z, the last letter, stands for 0. Thus: 40.

'Two brackets between two full stops is the symbol for a particular Paris street. They catalogued the whole of the capital. Every street, every passage, every dead-end was designated by a particular sign: ".( )." meant *street*. So then, what did the initial V stand for? The first street name that came to mind was *Vaugirard*. That turned out to be a correct assumption.

'Now for the last sign in the lower right corner. This one gave me a lot more trouble, and I only worked it out by racking my brains for a long time. After an eternity of trial and error, what finally dawned on me was what I should have thought of from the outset: the sign meant *Louis*.

'So now are you ready for the complete phrase? Here it is:

….(signed) *Red Bomber*

P.S. Write to me care of *Little Dagger*, 40 Rue de Vaugirard; I'm using the name Louis

'I needed to verify my deductions. Number 40 Rue de Vaugirard is the Hôtel du Renard Bleu. I disguised myself as best I could—as you can see, I have a certain talent in this area—and proceeded to walk up and down on the pavement opposite the hotel, watching carefully who came in and who came out.

'After about half an hour I saw a man approaching, a plump, heavy-jowled little man with an unintelligent face, whom I recognised immediately as my old client Jules Lanseigne, also known as *Little Dagger*.

'The ex-thief, out of prison for the last two years, had chosen the profession of innkeeper to rehabilitate himself in society.

'He went in to the hotel, I followed him, and as he was about to climb the stairs, I tapped him on the shoulder.

'He turned, startled, asked me in a gruff voice:

'"What do you want of me?"

'"You are indeed Jules Lanseigne?"

He looked at me from under lowered eyebrows.

'"Yes," he replied hesitantly. "Why do you ask?"

'"There's something I have to tell you. Can you spare me a few minutes?"

'The innkeeper, whom I knew to be a coward, paled visibly and looked as though he might try to escape. My black suit and the great beard adorning my chin made him think I was a refugee from the streets of Jerusalem.

'To prevent him getting away I took him by the arm, opened the door to the small ground floor room, and, after locking myself in the room with him, put the key in my pocket.

'His teeth were chattering. I looked at him out of the corner of my eye, and when I saw him try to reach under his jacket, I said:

'"Take care! You know that I know who you are because I called you by your real name. I know that you're very adept with a dagger and that, on the 18th of August, 1832, you were sentenced to only five years in prison due to lack of proof."

'I took a small revolver out of my pocket.

'"Sit here," I continued, placing a chair at one end of the table.

'I sat down at the other end of the table, placing my pistol in front of me.

'"And now," I said to him, "let's talk."'

10

'He sat down more dead than alive. He kept looking alternately at the gun and at me with an expression both fearful and ferocious.

'"You see," I continued calmly, "you're in my hands. You can't run away and you can't get rid of me by force. This little beauty in my hand can put a bullet in your head noiselessly before you can even cry for help. I don't want to have to hurt you, but you must answer every question I ask. Tell me the names of everyone staying in the hotel."

'"How do I know?" he growled, shrugging his shoulders without looking at me. "Let me look at my register. So many come here, they stay a day or two, and then they leave. I can't be expected to know everyone's name by heart."

'"So, I'm going to have to jog your memory. First of all, who do you have on the third floor?"

'"I've no idea."

'"Is it a woman?"

'"No."

'"A single man?"

'He hesitated for a moment.

'"Yes."

'"And you've no idea who he is?"

'"A commercial traveller, I think. He arrived yesterday evening."

'"Good. And the second floor?"

'"A law student. An employee at the Luxembourg."

'"Is that all?"

'"Yes."

'"Perfect. And who's on the first floor?"

'"A piano teacher."

'"Is that all?"

'"Yes."

'"You're lying."

'The innkeeper's ruddy face went pale.

'"You're going to tell me the name of the guest whose presence you're trying to hide."

'"Do you want to look at the register?"

'"No, I want you to talk. I'm not letting you out of here. I know you; you'll try to escape."

'The innkeeper squirmed on his chair. My unwavering stare appeared to be torture to him.

'"I told you I wanted a response."

'"And if I don't want to do it?"

'I picked up the revolver and pointed it at him.

'"I'm going to kill you like a dog,' I replied coldly.

'He gave a frightened start, but then looked at me with the insolence of a typical Parisian.

'"You wouldn't dare," he said. "I'm not afraid of your threats. You're trying to frighten me. A gunshot makes too much noise. No, you wouldn't dare to fire."

'"Just watch," I said with the same calm, indicating one of the faded roses blooming on the wallpaper. "Do you see that flower?"

'I pointed my revolver at the wall, there was a noise barely louder than the cracking of a whip, and the rose was covered with a black powder.

'"That powder is from a bullet," I said, getting up, "and if you don't tell me, I'll pierce your heart just like I pierced that flower and with just as little noise. For the last time, are you going to answer me?"

'The innkeeper had gone deathly pale. His bluster had been replaced by abject terror.

'He opened his mouth to speak, but suddenly stopped and instead beat his fist on the table.

'"No!" he cried, "I can't do it."

'"You can't do it, eh! You refuse to reply. Well, I know the man's name. He's the brother of the miserable wretch that appeared in court with you and escaped in Toulon. His name is Joseph Pichet."

'"It's not true," exclaimed Lanseigne, who was no longer frowning. "His name is Louis Ringard."

'Lanseigne's reply proved that my trick had worked.

'I had guessed correctly. *Louis* was the code name of the gangster. With one bound I was next to the innkeeper and had seized him by the collar, turned him round and pushed him into a corner of the room. Before he could recover from the shock, I had left the room and double-locked the door behind me.

'I rushed home to take off my disguise and continue my investigation.'

Maximilien had been so agitated during his account that he now had to stop for a moment to catch his breath.

'So,' I said, after a moment's silence, 'according to you, the crime was committed by the ringleader of the gang?'

'I don't know... I don't know,' he replied rather sharply. 'For now I'm trying to reconstruct the events; I'll work out the consequences later.

'One fact I do know: a letter signed by Red Bomber was found in M. Bréhat-Kerguen's room.

'Without wasting a moment, I resumed my investigation. I bought some peasant's clothes from a second-hand shop, shaved off my moustache, cut my hair, and covered my head with a blond wig.

'An hour later, I rang the doorbell of the Bréhat-Lenoir residence.

'M. Prosper opened the door; he didn't recognise me.

'"What do you want?" he asked, in a tone which showed me that he observed the rules of polite society far less with his inferiors than with his superiors.

'"I'm looking for work," I replied, with the most inane look I could muster, "and I'd like a valet position."

'"Have you done that kind of thing before?"

'"Yes, in the provinces."

'"Ah, the provinces. I don't much like people from the provinces. What makes you think that M. Bréhat-Kerguen is going to take the first servant that turns up? He's been well schooled by his poor brother, my late lamented master."

'"But," I insisted, "surely I can see him?"

'"You can come back whenever you want, as far as I'm concerned, but he's always coming and going, so you'll be hard pressed to meet him, I warn you."

'"All right, I'll come back," I said, shaking my head and sighing loudly. "It's really hard to make a living, these days."

'Just as I was about to leave, the doorbell rang loudly.

'"Ah! Wait," said the steward clutching hold of the bell cord, "This will be M. Bréhat-Kerguen, no doubt."

'And it was indeed he. You probably remember we saw him briefly as he walked past the windows of the drawing room the day of the autopsy.

'M. Bréhat-Kerguen must be about fifty years old. He is heavily built, with a bull neck, remarkably long arms, and huge hands covered in hair.

'There's something savage and primitive about him. It's obvious that he's always lived away from towns, in his country house in Brittany surrounded by heather, like a pig in its sty.

'His grey hair is always tousled. One lock of darker hair falls diagonally across his brow to join thick black eyebrows hiding very shrewd grey eyes. He has a ruddy complexion and thick lips and he sports a close-cropped beard. When he walks, he drags his left leg slightly. He is an altogether ugly person.

'He noticed me straight away.

'"Hmmph!" he growled at the manservant, sounding just like a bear. "Who's that?"

'M. Prosper bowed three or four times and explained why I was there.

'"A servant?" replied the Breton, shrugging his shoulders. "And what would I do with another servant? I already have more than I need. Servants!"

'He turned his back on us and started to climb the stairs. I was beginning to doubt the success of my venture when M. Bréhat-Kerguen, changing his mind, stopped on the stairs and called to me without turning round:

'"In fact, why not? Come with me."

'I followed him. When we got to the second floor, he pulled a key from his pocket and inserted it in the keyhole. He jiggled the bolt five or six times before he opened the door, as if to make sure that nobody had entered in his absence. Then he pushed the door open and, once I was inside, locked the door behind us.

'I found myself in a very modest room that overlooked the courtyard.

'In front of the window a writing table; at the rear of the room a large four-poster bed, a couple of chairs and two armchairs covered in velvet: that was the furniture. Near the chimney was a leather trunk.

'It was while ferreting around behind the trunk that M. Prosper had found the note from Red Bomber.

'M. Bréhat-Kerguen opened the window, pulled back the curtains which had been half closed, and let daylight into the room.

'He placed a chair in front of the window.

'"Sit there," he said.

'He placed himself with his back to the light and started to question me about my past, my habits, my family, etc., etc., with all the attention to detail of an experienced examining magistrate. But I had carefully prepared a story that I reeled out in great detail without hesitating or stopping; and the more specific his questions became, the more my mind, over-stimulated by the situation, supplied me with firm responses in keeping with the role I was playing.

'He seemed satisfied with the interview, for, having thought for a few moments while pacing up and down the room, he stopped in front of me and said:

'"Good. I'll take you into my service. We're leaving for Brittany as soon as possible. Go downstairs and tell the steward to come and speak to me."

'I had the job!'

11

'Three days later, I became aware through M. Prosper – who treated me with a sort of haughty pity and gave me sage advice each time my rustic *naïveté* aroused his master's wrath – I became aware, as I said, through that honest manservant, that the seals to M. Bréhat-Kerguen's room were going to be removed at his request and that of M. Castille, they being the dead man's two closest relatives.

'In fact, that evening around eight o'clock the crown prosecutor arrived, accompanied by his clerk, to carry out the operation and take an inventory.

'I had been waiting for that moment with an indescribable impatience. I was at last going to be able to get into the room where the crime had taken place. I was going to achieve at least part of the goal for which I had donned my tiresome disguise. After having studied the man from close up, I was now going to be able to do the same for the material objects.

'At eight o'clock precisely, M. Prosper said to me, with scarcely concealed chagrin:

'"My master is asking for you. The justice of the peace and M. Castille are here. I offered to help these gentlemen and shed light on various matters, but he told me to summon you. Take this lamp – not like that! You'll spill the oil, you imbecile. Go quickly, your master is waiting."

'M. Castille, the nephew of the deceased, had arrived along with the magistrate. As he shot a glance at the old Breton, I thought I detected a glimmer of joy, even though he tried to hide it.

'We went into the chamber where the autopsy had been held. The magistrate solemnly proceeded to remove the seals. After he had removed the last one, M. Bréhat-Kerguen could not suppress a sigh of satisfaction.

'The magistrate pulled the key, which had been given him for safe keeping, from his pocket and opened the door.

'"Please go first," he told me, "and light the way."

'The bedroom had been left as it was on the day of the crime. The bed was still unmade and the sheets were lying on the carpet.

'The room was on the corner of the house: its windows opened on the garden. I noticed they were solidly barred. Here, as well, the furniture was very simple and hardly reflected the dead man's immense fortune.

'The famous writing desk was a few steps away from the bed.

'All four people present headed towards that part of the room.

'"The testament still hasn't been found?" asked the magistrate in his nasal voice.

'"No," replied M. Castille, who seemed extremely upset and kept looking at M. Bréhat-Kerguen with barely concealed rage.

'The latter remained impassive.

'"Come! Let's take another look," said the magistrate. "Perhaps we'll have better luck this time."

'Was I mistaken? It seemed to me that an almost imperceptible smile flickered on the Breton's thick lips.

'Papers were turned over, and registers were opened and gone through with care. After an hour of searching, we had found no word indicating the last wishes of M. Bréhat-Lenoir.

'"As you can see, monsieur," said the magistrate, "I've done everything in my power. It is now a matter of record that your uncle did not leave a will. I take it you have no knowledge that the deceased had any papers other than those that are here?"

'"No, monsieur," replied the heir, disappointed, his forehead beaded with sweat. "No, my uncle told me a thousand times that he put all his papers and all his gold in this desk."

'"Well, as far as the money is concerned," replied the magistrate, "we know where that went. But it's very strange that we can't find a will. In any case, half my task has been accomplished. I shall now proceed to take the inventory."

'The clerk approached one of the tables, placed a briefcase stuffed full of paper on it and stood ready, his pen over his ear and his nose in the air, to take down his chief's instructions.

'At that moment, I noticed M. Bréhat-Kerguen—whom I was watching like a hawk—look anxiously towards the fireplace. It was over in a moment, and he immediately resumed his air of indifference.

'I followed the direction of his look.

'The dead man's watch, a superb gold Bréguet decorated with gemstones, was hanging on a nail by the fireplace.

'"Well, there's a rum burglar," I thought. "He kills a man in order to break into his writing desk, where he knows there are only a few pieces of gold, and fails to make off with a watch worth three thousand francs…"

'We started by taking an inventory of the furniture: table, chairs, armchairs, etc.

"'Let's have a look at the curtains," said the magistrate, moving towards the windows. "Give us some light, boy. Hmm, they're silk damask."

'The little clerk raised his head.

"'I rather think they're wool damask," he said. "My father and my uncle used to sell it; I should know."

'A discussion arose on this important matter between the master and his clerk.

'While it was going on, I observed the windows. They were, as I said previously, solidly barred; what's more, the catch was secured by a big padlock. "Well, he didn't come in that way," I told myself.

'A careful examination of the carpet touching the right-hand window, I thought I saw splashes of mud (I don't know if you remember, but it rained heavily on January 2, and afterwards there was a deep freeze.) It appeared as though someone had hidden himself behind the curtains, close to the window, for a while.

'I made a mental note.

'It was the justice of the peace who won the argument, the clerk conceding that there might be slightly more silk than wool in the curtains.

"'Now," said the magistrate, continuing with the inventory, "let's not forget the carpet. Here, boy," he said, talking to me, "place the lamp on the floor."

'I did as he asked and, after a few seconds of close examination, I noticed the faint, almost imperceptible trace of a footprint outlined in yellowish sand on the carpet.

'The footprint went in a direction from the windows to the bed.

"'Good," said the prosecutor. "A very ordinary carpet. Really, for a millionaire, it's rather modest. And the bed: walnut, but what a size! Look, monsieur," he added, turning towards M. Bréhat-Kerguen, "your brother, who was so afraid of burglars, slept in a bed under which a whole army of brigands could have hidden."

'It seemed to me that the old Breton's bushy eyebrows twitched at these remarks, made so casually by the magistrate.

'We went on to do the inventory of the items around the fireplace.

'Imagine my surprise when I looked across at the nail from which the watch had been hanging: the Bréguet was no longer there!

'And yet I had never let M. Bréhat-Kerguen out of my sight.

'After half an hour the inventory of the bedroom was complete and we went on to the other rooms in the residence.

'By eleven o'clock, everything was finished.'

12

'I had not yet found out why M. Bréhat-Kerguen had decided to take me into his service,' continued Maximilien, after a brief respite.

'Up to that point, he had only ever given me one order (when he told me to come up to help the prosecutor and bring the lamp.) Apart from that single occasion, he seemed to have completely forgotten my existence.

'I was, however, going to discover the reason the day after the inventory.

'That day, around seven o'clock, I met M. Prosper whose little face expressed the most profound discontent.

'"Would you believe," he said, "he's sending me to deliver this letter somewhere near the Bastille. He didn't want to use a courier, the old miser. He wants me to go myself, and straight away. In this weather, with all the snow and ice, I'm sure I shall fall sick."

'He started to walk away, muttering to himself, when he turned abruptly and said:

'"I almost forgot. He wants to see you right away. Go right up."

'I found my old Breton in his dressing-gown, with a scarf wrapped around his head, smoking a rather large pipe.

'"Get a broom and a duster," he said haughtily, "and come with me."

I brought the equipment he had demanded. We went down one floor and entered the dead man's bedroom.

'"It's all in a terrible state," my master growled, casting his eye on the disorder. "You will put everything back in place, sweep up, and dust. And quickly, do you understand? Start with the carpet."

'He pulled on the window cords. In the light of day, the traces of the footprint were even more clearly visible. M. Bréhat-Kerguen appeared to notice it at the same time I did. He quickly closed the curtain.

'"Sweep the carpet first, and be careful about it."

'And, since I carried out the work as slowly and clumsily as I could, the old Breton's face turned crimson and he let out a forceful curse.

'"Faster than that. I told you I was in a hurry. Ah," he continued in a lower voice, "if I could bend down, if I didn't have this damned pain in my kidneys, I would have finished the job myself a while ago.'

'I had got as far as the bed. M. Bréhat-Kerguen seemed to hesitate for a moment.'

'"Sweep under the bed," he said, curtly.

'As I bent over, I quickly understood his hesitancy in giving me the order, for I saw, under the bed, two spots of the yellowish powder I had observed near the windows and elsewhere in the bedroom.

'Someone had hidden under the bed. The marks had been made by two boot heels. And note this: they were at the head of the bed, which confirmed and explained an observation I had made earlier and which I will talk about later.

'As you can well imagine, I was very careful not to erase such vital clues.

'"Now," my master said when I had finished, "you'll take the sheets and have them cleaned as soon as possible. I don't care to keep a dead man's linen any longer than I have to."

'It seemed to me that he took the death of his own brother with cynical indifference.

'I collected the sheets, rolled them up, and tucked them under my arm.

'"You can go now," ordered M. Bréhat-Kerguen. "I'll take care of the writing desk myself."

'I went straight up to the room that had been assigned to me, and after double-locking the door, I wasted no time in examining the sheets I had brought with me.'

Here, the philosopher interrupted his account once again. He appeared tired and I told him so.

'Yes,' he admitted to me, 'I feel I may be close to another breakdown. I am unbelievably tired. For over a week, I've been pushing my brain beyond the limit: I've only given you a brief summary of what I've done. If you only knew how many days and nights I've spent working everything out and finding a solution. I only hope I can hold out until the end.'

Then, after a moment's silence, he asked:

'Would you happen to have a glass of *eau-de-vie* ? I've a feeling it would do me a power of good.'

I opened my liqueur cabinet and served him. He drank three glasses of rum in quick succession, then gave out a deep sigh and lay back in the armchair.

'I must confess,' I said, facing him from a spot close to the fireplace, 'that your account throws me into confusion. I feel as though I'm in a magical dream that is creating bizarre silhouettes before my eyes. Just now, your main suspect seemed to be the mastermind of the old gang. Now you seem to be accusing M. Bréhat-Kerguen of fratricide.'

There was the flicker of a smile as the philosopher opened his eyes.

'Patience,' he said. 'You're not yet at the end of your dream, nor I of my story. You'll soon have more surprising news.

'I haven't yet told you about Dr. Wickson. It's time to address that matter.

'Let us, if you will, go back to the day of the autopsy. I already expressed my opinion that you and the authorities had been fooled by a clever trick.

'But I haven't yet shared with you another more recent discovery which settles the matter beyond doubt. I noticed that, each time he approached the body, the first thing the Indian doctor did was to move the bed sheet to cover up the dead man's feet.

'You naturally didn't notice this from where you stood, but I did, and I immediately decided to clear the matter up.

'Two hours later, on the same day – roughly two hours after I had left you – I went back to the Bréhat-Lenoir residence and, using the excuse with M. Prosper that you had forgotten an important paper and had sent me to fetch it, I was able to re-enter the chamber where the body lay.

'I went over to the corpse and lifted up the sheet where it covered the feet.

'The first thing that struck me was the strange shape of the body's lower limbs.

'One ankle joint was swollen by a lump the size of an egg.

'A quick examination revealed that there was a black mark on the heel of the right foot, surrounded by a violet circle.

'As I hadn't got a minute to lose, I took out a pocket knife and made an incision in that spot. from whence I drew several drops of a brown liquid mixed with blood which collected in my watch case.

'As soon as I got home, I analysed the liquid. As you know, I studied chemistry (indeed, which subject had I not studied, you may well ask?) but I was unable to recognise the substance I had gathered.

'Nonetheless, I didn't give up.

'I bought a live rabbit and, with a drop of the unknown liquid on the tip of a needle, I made a small injection in its paw.

'It died within ten seconds, as if struck by lightning.

'At long last, I had identified the instrument of the crime.

'It was curare, the subtle poison that South American Indians make from plants and mix with snake venom. It can kill with frightening speed.

'The murderer hid under the bed, waiting for the victim to fall asleep. Then, when he judged the time ripe, he slid the killing needle between the sheets and injected into the victim's heel a poison a thousand times more deadly than a dagger to the heart.

'Here we have another established fact, confirmed by a small bloodstain that I found on the sheets at a spot where the dead man's feet had been. As you can see, we're a long way from the original theory of arsenic.

'As far as I'm concerned, the killer isn't poor Guérin, it's M. Bréhat-Kerguen and I could have him arrested tomorrow with the proof I've discovered. But I want to go further still.

'And because every crime must have a motive in order for the judges to sentence the criminal, I shall prove that the crime wasn't about a few pieces of gold but the disappearance of a will and the consequent theft of three million francs.'

13

Maximilien Heller's story had impressed me greatly.

I admired his marvellous clarity of thought, his confident and penetrating observations, and the passion for the truth that had led my strange friend to insert himself into the murderer's entourage so as to spy on his movements and his gestures and even penetrate his thoughts.

I told him enthusiastically how impressed I was with his efforts.

'Don't congratulate me too soon,' he replied with a self-deprecating smile. 'I haven't finished yet. I know the killer and I know the method. But there still remain three questions: How did the murderer get into the victim's room? What is the connection between M. Bréhat-Kerguen and Red Bomber? What interest does Dr. Wickson have in the crime? I should know the answers to the first two eventually, but as for the third, I want to solve it as soon as possible. Time is against me, for I have to work it out before I leave Paris.'

'What? You're leaving?'

'Obviously, I have to accompany my "master" to Brittany.'

'What day would that be?'

'I don't know exactly, but I believe M. Bréhat-Kerguen has very good reasons for leaving as soon as possible—maybe tomorrow or the day after. So you can see there's no time to lose. I came to find you because you can help me lift one corner of the veil that still hides the truth.'

'Me?' I asked, surprised.

'Yes, I need to ask you a small favour, and that preamble, which you may have found rather long, served as an introduction to my request.'

'Ask away, my dear friend, I'll be only too happy to oblige and assist in any way I can in the success of your courageous venture.'

'You are, I believe, related to the Countess of Bréant?'

'Yes, she's my cousin, a charming woman. I hope you don't suspect her of being mixed up in the crime?' I said, laughingly.

'Well, in fact,' said Maximilien, with a smile, 'she may be a little bit complicit.'

'Really? You have me worried.'

'Tell me, is she throwing a ball tonight?'

'Yes. She's even invited me, but I can't go.'

'I'm sorry. Not only are you going to the ball, you're going to introduce me.'

'What? You want—.'

'That surprises you, doesn't it? Well, when you hear that Dr. Wickson is one of the guests, you'll begin to understand.'

'And you want to continue your observations?'

'Precisely. And if dressing up as a servant to advance my cause hasn't deterred me, neither will dressing up as a dancer.'

'You dance?'

'Like a *débutante's* suitor. So, it's agreed?'

'Absolutely. Come round at ten o'clock. I'll be happy to present you to my pretty cousin.'

'Many thanks,' said Maximilien, getting up and shaking my hand.

'But how are you going to get away this evening?'

'M. Bréhat-Kerguen goes to bed every night at nine o'clock. I have the key to the garden and the street. I can come and go as I wish.'

'Until tonight, then.'

'Until tonight.'

14

At around ten o'clock, the philosopher arrived. I didn't recognise him at first because his disguise was no less perfect than that he had worn earlier in the day.

He had taken great care in his dress. A black evening jacket accentuated his height. His hair had been carefully curled; a thin moustache decorated his upper lip. His normally stern features now wore the smilingly fatuous expression affected by men who spend their entire life in social gatherings. A large camellia blossomed on his chest.

'Well?' he said, as he held out his hand. 'What do you think of my new outfit?'

'You're the most extraordinary man I know, and I'm grateful to you in advance for the effusive thanks I shall get from my cousin for having brought such a perfect dancing partner.'

'Good for you. I hope I look the part. You're finding it difficult to recognise the poor wretch you saw a fortnight ago, wavering between his cat and his hot-water bottle. Unfortunately,' he added with a sigh, 'I'm no less feeble and sick than I was then. I know full well that all my energy comes from pure willpower and I sense there will be a terrible price to pay later on. My only desire is to be able to finish my task. And then—come what may—I'll go back and die in my attic. But I see you're ready. Let's go. I'm like a dog in the hunt, and I don't want to lose sight of my quarry.'

My little cousin, the Comtesse de Bréant, was typical of the accomplished Parisienne: slender, elegant, delicate, and worldly.

She had been married for eighteen months and was not yet twenty years old.

Her husband was the Comte de Bréant, and it was a marriage of affection. He was an exceedingly rich gentleman of excellent family who had sown his wild oats in his youth and, upon reaching middle age, had gathered up the tattered shreds of his heart and offered them to the most beautiful young woman imaginable .

They were a charming couple. Edile loved her husband because he was elegant and distinguished, had made her a countess, and gave her the richest fineries and the prettiest jewels. In a word, he satisfied her every whim with the inexhaustible tenderness with which a father spoils his beloved child.

The Comte de Bréant loved his darling Edile because this new life, starting at middle age, filled him with inexpressible joy and it was due to her that he had finally found happiness. Whenever she passed, brilliant and dazzling, through the golden salons that she animated with her gaiety and youth, he watched her with that soft and melancholy joy that the voyager, tired and disillusioned of trips to far-off lands, feels contemplating the steeple of his village church and the native soil he never should have left.

She loved her world, because she reigned over it as its adored queen. The count, who had no other desire than to please his wife, and no pleasures other than hers, flung his salon doors wide and, as long as his little queen was the most beautiful, the most admired, and the most applauded woman there, he was happy.

That caused other men to shrug their shoulders.

'Oh, cousin,' Edile said to me as she sat down and took both my hands in hers, 'how good of you to have brought us such a marvellous dancer. I've just waltzed with him and I've never felt so light. I seemed to have wings on my shoulders. Tell me, is he staying long in Paris?'

'No, my dear Edile, he's leaving in a couple of days, and I'm sure he'll be full of regret, once he hears the excellent opinion you have of him.'

She gave a little pout and disappeared in a chiffon cloud.

Maximilien sought me out five minutes later. He smiled to learn of the enthusiasm he had inspired in the mistress of ceremonies, then lowered his voice:

'Here he is,' he said. 'Look out.'

And indeed Dr. Wickson had just made his entrance into one of the salons.

The Comte de Bréant hastened to meet him and shook his hand effusively. The doctor had saved the life of one of the count's sisters ten years ago, and he had not forgotten.

As word spread throughout the salons that Dr. Wickson had arrived, everyone wanted to get close to the man who had at one time been so celebrated. His marvellous cures had caused such a stir in Paris that, even after ten years, people had not forgotten.

The dancing stopped, and people pressed forward to see him.

He smiled discreetly and walked into the middle of the brilliant crowd with the haughty air of a conqueror. The count presented Edile, to whom he made an elaborate bow and proceeded to the gaming room.

The gaming tables had been set out in an elegant greenhouse that the count had commissioned for his darling Edile, and which opened out on to the salons.

The players were installed behind banks of rhododendrons, camellias, and azaleas. The rest of the greenhouse had been allocated to the dancers. From time to time one could see, though the light-drenched foliage, an elegant couple seeking a moment of rest and freshness in the midst of the artificial spring.

Dr. Wickson went to one of the gaming tables. As he leant forward to sit down, he was unable to suppress a slight cry of pain.

'Are you suffering, doctor?' enquired his partner, who was none other than our old acquaintance, the public prosecutor, M. Ribeyrac. 'My God, yes,' replied the Englishman, nodding his head. "I have sharp pains in my kidneys. Ah, monsieur, we doctors take care of those close to us, but as for curing ourselves, we're the last to notice anything.'

I noticed a slight rustling of the leaves of a large rhododendron just behind the doctor. Maximilien had taken up his post.

I went back into the salon.

My friend, M. Robert Cernay, had just arrived. He was the centre of attraction of a group of mothers who appeared very agitated. There were several young women in the group and one could hear them clamouring from all sides:

'A tale of brigands! How charming. Please tell us.'

'No,' said Robert gaily, defending himself. 'It would keep you awake for at least a dozen nights.'

'But, monsieur,' replied a beautiful young girl with blonde hair, 'our mothers asked you to.'

'Yes, yes, monsieur, do tell them,' implored my cousin, joining in. 'These ladies are a little tired and it would be a charming break.'

'Your slightest wish is my command, madam,' replied Robert to the little mistress of the house, 'and I shall begin forthwith.'

'Ah!' cried the joyful chorus.

And all those pretty eyes glittered with pleasure, such was the attraction of brigand stories to the ladies.

15

'I must warn you, ladies,' Robert started, 'don't expect comic-opera brigands, with their cocked hats with feathers, their soft boots and their waxed moustaches. My man—for the band comprised a single man—had not a shred of poetry in his soul, I swear.

'He was a heavy individual, very vulgar, a sort of badly-licked bear wrapped in a greatcoat covered in fur. His face was hidden by a thick scarf and a cap pulled down over his eyes.

'Last Thursday, I was walking along Rue de l'Université; it must have been about ten o'clock at night. I had heard heavy and uneven steps behind me for a while when I was suddenly seized by the arm.

'"Don't move and don't shout for help," a low voice said rapidly. "It would be useless and I don't mean you any harm."

'I tried to break free, but the stranger held my arm in a vice-like grip.

'"I have a small favour to ask,' continued the strange individual. I know who you are, I know you have a considerable fortune. You're not going to refuse to lend me five hundred francs."

'"A plague on you. Be gone!" I replied, taking the man for an escapee from the local asylum. "Do you think I have that kind of money on me?"

'"What about that five hundred franc watch you bought yesterday at the Palais-Royal? And that diamond pin your aunt Ursula gave you at New Year?"

'I was dumbfounded.

'"It's just a bad joke at my expense," I said to myself.

'"You haven't a moment to lose," he replied. "I only wanted five hundred francs at first. But because you were uncooperative, you'll have to give me the watch and the pin as well."

'I heard a vehicle approaching.

'"I'm not giving you a centime," I said resolutely, "and if you don't leave immediately, I shall call the police."

'"Oh, the police!" he replied, with a rude laugh, "I'm very familiar with how they operate. Before they respond to your call, I'll have put you down on the pavement. You see, I'm not joking. Do as I say."

'The vehicle arrived at high speed. My assailant looked round anxiously. He let go of my arm and I caught a glimpse of a dagger. But before he had the time to use it on me, I charged him in the chest with my shoulder so violently, he was sent sprawling on the pavement. He let out a foul oath. I think I hurt him badly. Just at that moment the vehicle sped by, causing a diversion that allowed me to escape rapidly from the scene of the attack.'

Joyful laughter followed the end of my friend's story. Everyone congratulated him on the courage and presence of mind he had shown in such difficult circumstances.

Above the chorus of praise, a sharp, discordant voice could be heard, that of an old maid covered in jewels on whom the tale had made an extraordinary impression.

'It's dreadful!' she cried, holding a bottle of smelling salts under her long nose. 'Killings in the streets of Paris! Rue de l'Université, monsieur, is where I live. Oh, My God, I won't ever dare to go out again.'

They managed to calm the old maid, who appeared on the verge of a nervous breakdown. The dances started again and the ball recommenced in full swing.

I went over to the greenhouse. In the doorway of the last salon, I found Maximilien Heller.

'Well?" I asked him.

'He's a horrible cheat,' he replied in a low voice.

Then he hastened away to ask the Comtesse de Bréant for a dance, lest she notice his absence for the past hour.

I went into the greenhouse. There were three or four men standing around a gaming table, motionless, their gaze fixed on the green cloth.

I joined the spectators. After ten minutes, the Englishman reached out his large hand to the pile of gold to his left and, with an imperturbable calm, swept in into his pocket. His partner stood up. He was alarmingly pale. I heard him murmur in Dr. Wickson's ear:

'I shall have the honour to give you the rest tomorrow before noon, monsieur.'

The spectators looked at each other in astonishment. One of them said to me:

'That's the fifth hand he's lost. That devil of a doctor has beaten everyone he's played so far.'

Wickson looked around with his little grey eyes that gleamed like carbuncles and, in a voice filled with triumphant pride asked:

'Come, gentlemen, who will take his place? I hope you're not going to let me win like this all night? Surely there's one of you that will seek revenge.'

There was a moment of hesitation among the crowd.

'Come now,' repeated the doctor. 'Who'll sit down against me?'

'I will,' said a deep voice.

The crowd stood back and Maximilien Heller appeared.

He was very pale; his brow was furrowed and his eyes flashed with a dark fire. At that moment he looked like the wild and feverish man I had met the day I first set eyes on him.

The elegant dancer had given way to the avenger of Louis Guérin.

The Englishman frowned slightly and hid the surprise and disappointment he felt behind a forced smile.

'I hope, monsieur, that you will be skilful enough to overcome the bad luck that has dogged these gentlemen so far.'

Maximilien said nothing, but shot his adversary a look that was so cold and penetrating that the other blinked and his eyes reflected a certain anxiety.

Then the philosopher took the cards in his slender hands, shuffled them, examined them carefully, and counted them out one by one.

Another frown crossed Dr. Wickson's brow. The spectators looked at each other with some surprise.

'It's your turn to deal, monsieur,' said Maximilien, curtly, handing his adversary the pack.

The witnesses to the strange scene were experienced players whose hearts had become hardened and whose senses had become immune to the poignant emotions of the game. Nevertheless, the sight of these two men battling coldly and in silence, their glances clashing like brilliant blades, observing and studying each other with the attention and *sang-froid* of two athletes competing for the ultimate prize, presented a singularly compelling picture.

The battle lasted a quarter of an hour, which seemed to us like a century. The adversaries appeared to be of equal force. Each had scored four points. Eventually, Maximilien announced with a smile, and without taking his eyes off the Englishman:

'The king! I win!'

Dr. Wickson almost jumped out of his chair. A sigh of relief escaped the lips of all present and those who had bet claimed their winnings, while profusely thanking Maximilien Heller.

The philosopher bowed and turned to his opponent:

'Would you care for a rematch, monsieur?' he asked.

'No, thank you,' replied the doctor, standing up. 'I said I'd play until I was beaten. I'm leaving now.'

Just at that moment the Comte de Bréant arrived, looking worried.

'Ah,' he said, noticing that we were starting to leave the gaming table, 'I'm so glad to see you're stopping those blasted card games, my dear friends. I heard that Monsieur L… lost a considerable sum, and I was coming to ask you to put a brake on the ardour that, I fully confess, I feared might lead to deadly consequences.'

Dr. Wickson leaned towards the master of the house's ear.

'Rest assured,' he said in a low voice. 'It is I who won that sum. I wanted to teach that scatterbrain a lesson. You can trust me: there will be no repeat.'

The Comte de Bréant pumped the hand of the honest Englishman effusively.

'Tell me,' said the latter. 'What is the name of that tall, pale monsieur who is now walking towards the salon?'

'He's a charming fellow, apparently. He was introduced to us by my wife's cousin.'

'Ah. And his name?'

'His name is…my word. I don't remember.'

Dr. Wickson stared after the departing Maximilien with a terrifying look on his face.

16

We were having supper.

It was very late, so a great many of the dancers had already left. Only the intrepid remained: those who liked to see the arrival of dawn.

During supper, Dr. Wickson regaled us all with his lively and fascinating conversation.

He first told of a tiger hunt along the banks of the Ganges, then moved on to the extraordinary adventures that befell him during a trip he took in the Australian desert.

After that, he thrilled his audience with tales of Red Indians. Fenimore Cooper was all the rage and everyone wanted to know about the Sioux, the Pawnies, and the Delaware. The doctor's discourse was so captivating that al other conversation stopped.

In the hushed silence, the only voice that could be heard was that of the Englishman.

Later, after countless changes of topic, he ended up recounting some of the thousands of little stories that Parisians love to hear… about Monsieur So-and-So, Mademoiselle This-and-That, Madame Something-or-Other. This devil of a man seemed to know everything, and one could see, from his coy reticence, that he knew far more than he was saying.

He gave the impression of a sort of Comte de Saint-Germain. He had seen every country, met the most famous men in the four corners of the world, and even seemed – even more extraordinarily – to have lived in several countries at the same time.

Since he loved talking about himself and his heroic deeds more than anything else, it wasn't long before he talked about some of the celebrated operations he had performed.

The audience paid even greater attention.

'Yes, ladies and gentlemen,' he proclaimed, raising his voice, 'I'm quite certain that, by holding the hand of one of you in mine for a minute, I could not only tell what was ailing you but, at the same time, indicate the remedy.'

'It's incredible….it's astonishing,' came cries from all quarters.

They were about to ask the doctor to perform the experiment when Edile, who preferred the sound of an orchestra to that of the doctor's voice, and the petticoat to a medical conference, stood up and made her way to the salons. Everyone followed her.

As the dances restarted, a number of guests gathered round the doctor, each clamouring to get a sample of those finely-ground powders with their magical properties.

The Englishman listened attentively to each request.

'Oh, monsieur,' said the old lady with the jewels in a doleful voice, 'if you can discover what I'm suffering from, I'll proclaim you the best doctor in the world.'

'The reward is far too precious, mademoiselle,' the doctor replied gallantly, 'for me not to attempt to deserve it.'

The elderly spinster blushed and extended her thin hand to the Englishman, who appeared to concentrate for several seconds.

'Yes, you are indeed afflicted.'

'It's true, isn't it, monsieur?'

'Yes,' confirmed the doctor. 'You probably experience a general malaise, without being able to pinpoint a particular area.'

'That's exactly right, doctor. Exactly right.'

'Heart palpitations.'

'Oh, yes! Yes!'

'Well, I'm going to cure you,' replied the Englishman with his imperturbable aplomb.

He put his hand in his jacket pocket and pulled out a small paper packet.

'Take this powder twice a day,' he told her, 'and you'll be cured within a week.'

Edile approached the group.

'Now then, ladies,' she said in her most cheerful voice, clapping her hands, 'the gentlemen are waiting for you. A ball is not the place to listen to tales of adventure.'

The Comte de Bréant gave his wife a tender look which was meant to reproach her for the irreverent manner in which she had alluded to the science of their guest, the doctor. But Edile pretended not to notice and turned her back on him so charmingly that he couldn't help thinking he had the sweetest little wife in the world.

'Please excuse me, madame,' said Dr. Wickson, approaching her with an ingratiating smile. 'My humble science has seemingly interrupted your delightful festivities. I pray you will forgive me, so I shall not, as I travel to foreign lands, bear the burden of having displeased you.'

He offered her his hand.

'Look at the superb diamond ring on our hostess's finger,' whispered Maximilien, 'and observe how Dr. Wickson stares at it. She refuses to take his hand. That's very wise of her.'

I couldn't help laughing at his comment, and thinking that his prejudices were clouding his judgment.

'It's already three o'clock in the morning,' I noted. 'Shouldn't we be thinking of leaving?'

'Let's wait another few minutes,' he replied, without taking his eyes off the good doctor. 'It looks as though there's going to be some kind of denouement, and I'd like to be here for it.'

Maximilien Heller's prediction wasn't long in happening.

There was a sudden shrill cry and everyone turned to see where it came from. The bejewelled old spinster could be seen waving her scrawny arms and rolling her eyes.

'What happened?' asked everyone at once.

'What happened? My bracelet is lost. Lost! It must have come off and fallen under a bench. Oh, My God, I had it on less than half an hour ago.'

'Calm down,' said Edile, who was accustomed to loud noise. 'The staff will find it tomorrow and bring it back to you.'

'Oh, it's not just the value. It was a precious souvenir.'

'It was paste,' murmured my malicious cousin, who had come over and was now standing next to me.

A handsome woman with ample shoulders and dazzlingly pale arms approached Edile. She appeared very upset.

'As you can see, my dear, I'm worried stiff,' she confided in a half-whisper. 'You remember the diamond ring my husband gave me three years ago? I think I must have lost it when I took my glove off. I'd be most obliged if you could tell your servants to look for it and bring it back to me tomorrow.'

'My God!' shrieked another guest. 'I've lost my bracelet.'

'And I've lost my broach,' cried yet another.

'My watch!' shouted a corpulent gentleman who had spent the whole night at the buffet.

My poor little cousin had turned pale from the shock.

'This is the denouement I was talking about,' said the philosopher, taking me by the arm. 'There's not a minute to lose.'

Dr. Wickson was nowhere to be seen.

In the reception area we ran into the Comte de Bréant who was raking his butler over the coals.

'Can you believe it?' he said as he shook my hand. 'Five silver place sittings have vanished and cannot be found.'

We left the devastated premises and found a cab. Maximilien Heller said not a word during the journey. He appeared to be plunged in thought and I respected his silence.

Five minutes later, we pulled up in front of the Hôtel du Renard Bleu which was connected via a small door to the garden of the Bréhat-Lenoir residence.

17

The next day, in the afternoon, I received a letter that went as follows:

My dear Doctor,

Tonight we leave for Brittany. This morning M. Bréhat-Kerguen looked at me several times in a way that did not augur well. Then, after ordering me to go up to his room, he subjected me to an interrogation no less detailed and meticulous than the first. I again acquitted myself with honour, that is to say, by affecting once more a bovine stupidity.

Does he still harbour some suspicions? I would tend to believe the contrary for, after putting a host of questions to me, he announced that he would definitely take me into his service and I should therefore be ready to leave the next night for his residence in Brittany.

I regret not being able to say farewell to you in person, but my master keeps a very vigilant eye on me, and it's impossible for me to go out.

You have always treated my strange behaviour with such benevolence that I feel authorised to ask you for yet another favour.

I do not know how long I shall be away. Perhaps I shall never return! I wish to name you as the executor of my estate. I bequeath you all my books and papers. If I die burn the manuscripts without reading them. I particularly want you to destroy the pile of papers that I indicated to you in my bedroom on the left, which contain the history of my miserable life.

Goodbye once again. I shall write to you often to keep you up to date with everything I do and all I discover.

Please do the same whenever something new comes to your attention.

I shake your hand.

Maximilien Heller

I sat thoughtfully for a while after reading the missive, written in a firm hand. I had difficulty in understanding the peculiar method he had devised of attaching himself closely to the villain. What did he still hope to uncover? Wouldn't it have been much simpler and less dangerous to have simply gone to the police and let them solve the mystery and unravel the tangled skein?

Couldn't such a perilous undertaking blow up without warning? The string of disguises and the concealment of secrets at every turn seemed beyond the powers of a normal human being. Should M. Bréhat-Kerguen ever catch him out, or he incur the slightest suspicion, he would be dead. He would be completely at the other's mercy in the remote Brittany residence, and the murderer wouldn't stop at one more crime to protect himself. And, if Maximilien Heller were to die, the hard-won framework of proof so painstakingly assembled would die with him and Louis Guérin would climb the steps of the scaffold.

In accordance with Maximilien Heller's wishes, I went to his attic and made an enormous package of his books and manuscripts and ordered them to be brought to my premises. I separated the pile of papers that constituted his memoirs and placed it in the drawer of my writing desk.

PART II

1

For the rest of the story, I shall let Maximilien Heller speak.

Almost every day he sent me his diary and his observations. I conserved them and now publish them in chronological order without changing any of the content, in order to give an accurate picture of the character of that strange philosopher.

Chartres, 17 January

We left yesterday around eight o'clock. The weather was awful. The storm rumbled with such intensity that I wasn't able to sleep a wink the whole night. M. Bréhat-Kerguen had hired a coach and ordered me to sit next to him. He didn't take his eyes off me for a second. Yesterday I was obliged to employ a ruse in order to post the letter I had written. This morning, my master, who seemed overcome by fatigue, threw himself down on a bed in the inn and I dashed off a letter to you, fearful that he could awaken at any moment

Do not reply to me before the 25th of the month. At that time, you can address your letters to the postmaster at Loc-ahr (near Loc-nevinen). I'll always find a way to reach him and collect my letters.

I would like to know, above all, whether Dr. Wickson is still in Paris and if there is any news of thefts as audacious as that of which the de Bréants were victim.

Speaking of which, when you next see your pretty cousin, tell her not to worry. The five silver table settings that were stolen and the rings, bracelets, watches, etc. of the victims will all be returned to their owners, before—.

The letter stopped there abruptly. Undoubtedly M. Bréhat-Kerguen woke up just at that moment and Maximilien never found the time to finish his epistle.

I found the information the philosopher had asked for. Dr. Wickson was no longer in Paris and there had been no more reports of thefts and nocturnal attacks.

Kerguen, 22 January

Kerguen manor is situated on the edge of a large pine forest, two kilometres from the village of Loc-ahr. It is an ancient construction close to ruin, with high walls blackened by the centuries and pierced by small windows whose bluish glass is encased in lead.

There is something sinister and fantastic about this old residence. It's like a tomb rising from the dark foliage of the fir trees.

A deathly silence reigned. We arrived in the dead of night by a road that had been broken up by the snow.

My master got out first and knocked several times on the iron gate, swearing profusely – the only words I had heard him pronounce during the entire journey. A peasant, half asleep, came to open the door for us.

It was the gardener, a near-idiot who only understood about three words of French and who seemed to possess the passive obedience of the brute animal.

We walked across the garden, which is very big, and arrived in a small badly-paved courtyard at the other side of which were steps leading up to the front entrance of the dismal residence.

The very moment that M. Bréhat-Kerguen set foot in the courtyard, a deep growl was heard from the darkest corner.

My master turned quickly round.

'Ah, Jacquot, you're awake,' he said with a loud laugh. 'That's a good boy, you recognise people and greet them. How are you, my old friend?'

So saying, he went to the corner from whence the beast's growl had emanated. Despite the darkness, I could make out a large iron cage that cut off the corner of the courtyard and, behind the bars, a huge brown mass that moved slowly.

I heard the noise of an iron gate opening and, by moving forward a few steps, could see my master enter the cage and hug a gigantic bear in his arms.

The animal let out small growls of pleasure.

The touching scene lasted about a minute.

'Hum!' muttered my master after he separated from his wild friend. 'Jacquot is a good boy when you know him, but if anyone else were to visit him, he would tear them apart with his teeth.'

His remarks appeared to be addressed to me. But, since I had no intention of ever visiting Jacquot, I was not cowed by the threat.

M. Bréhat-Kerguen went up the front steps and dismissed the gardener, who lived in a small hovel next to the garden gate.

He opened the lock with a large key; the door swung open on squeaky hinges, and closed with a thud that shook the ancient foundations.

The lord of the manor took a lantern from one wall and lit it.

We found ourselves in a long corridor, at the end of which could be seen a wide stone staircase.

'Follow me!' ordered M. Bréhat-Kerguen in a harsh voice.

We went up two flights of stairs. The rooms of the old manor seemed to me to be bizarrely distributed.

Two narrow corridors stretched on either side of the landing, from which doors opened at regular intervals.

The place looked like a convent with its dark corridors and its cells.

'This is your room,' said M. Bréhat-Kerguen, pushing open one of the small doors and showing me a damp and badly-furnished room. 'You'll find wood in the corner.'

He shone the light from the lantern in my face and his little grey eyes examined me attentively.

'You're in my service,' he said, stressing every word. 'You have to be ready to obey me every moment of the day or the night. Your work will not be very tiring. But I forbid you to set foot beyond the garden walls. I hold unlimited rights over you, and if you disobey me in this matter, I will punish you with my own hands. On the other hand, if you obey me in everything you will be rewarded in a way that nobody else will match, believe me.'

As he pronounced the last words, his look was even more piercing than before. Then he turned abruptly and walked out.

2

Other than the gardener of whom I already spoke and who is undoubtedly retarded, M. Bréhat-Kerguen has only one other servant, an aged housekeeper who does not understand a word of French. My master eats prodigiously and drinks even more. His wine, by the way, is excellent.

After his meal, which he took at midday, he locked himself in his rooms on the first floor. Meanwhile, I took a walk in the garden which is very well laid out and lined with superb *espaliers*.

Crossing the small courtyard, I could see Jacquot lying stretched out the length of his cage, warming himself in the pale January sunshine.

He is a magnificent black bear with, it appears, ferocious instincts. He was holding a side of meat between his huge paws and was eating it with a gluttony that gave cause for thought.

Seeing me walk past, he lifted his great head and gave a deep growl.

I walked in the garden for about an hour, racking my brains for a way in which I could arrange for the letters I intend to write every day to reach you.

The walk in the fresh air did me a world of good. My mind was working furiously and the north wind, which was blowing violently, refreshed me.

When I get back to Paris, I shall start taking cold showers.

I took advantage of the hour's walk to make a careful examination of the sombre residence.

The façade has eight windows.

I had no difficulty recognising the window of my room because, to facilitate my investigation, I had left it open. It is the third from the right on the second floor.

From what little information I was able to extract from the gardener, I am led to believe the master's apartment is below the room I have been allocated.

In front of the manor is a beautiful Norwegian fir that almost reaches the Gothic window of my room.

I walked all the way around the house; on the south side, all the shutters were closed. Apparently these apartments have never been occupied.

I was just about to go back inside the manor, when something shiny caught my eye; it was proceeding slowly along the length of the orchard wall. You know I am very sharp-eyed.

I approached it quietly, keeping close to the *espaliers*, in pursuit of this new mystery.

In this part of the garden there is a beautifully clear fish-pond whose banks touch the wall at a point where it has slightly deteriorated.

I waited and watched for five minutes.

All of a sudden, there was a commotion in the water, sending circular waves one after the other across the pond, and I saw a superb trout leap out of its element and land on the wall, its scales glistening as it thrashed about.

Don't for a minute think that I am telling a tall tale; it was not long before the phenomenon was explained.

The trout dangled above the pond, held in suspension by a thin string. By following the thread with my naked eye, I noticed two skinny little hands reaching over the wall and hauling the fish up on the line.

I advanced softly and, going up on my toes, I grasped the hands of the unknown fisherman in mine.

A startled cry came from the other side of the wall, and I saw the frightened little face of a twelve year old child appear between the moss-covered stones, his face daubed and his hair ash-blond.

'Don't hurt me, monsieur,' said the child in bad French and an imploring voice. 'I promise I won't do it again.'

'I've got you, you little thief. What would M. Bréhat-Kerguen say if he knew you were fishing for his trout?'

But, because I wanted to make an ally of this little man, I didn't look fierce or speak in too rough a voice. And he, with the perspicacity that children possess to such a rare degree, quickly realised that I wasn't an ogre about to eat him.

The expression of terror on his face was quickly replaced by one of naïve astonishment.

He stared at me for several seconds, then asked abruptly:

'Is this your first time here?'

'Yes.'

'Are you a friend of M. Bréhat-Kerguen?'

'Not exactly.'

'Who are you then?'

'Try and guess.'

I had let go of his hands. He crouched down, pressed his rosy cheeks against his closed fists, and looked me up and down, a look of surprise in his wide blue eyes.

'Who are you? Bless me, I don't know. Did you come from Paris with him?

'Yes.'

'Ah! So you're Parisian?'

He looked at me more keenly. He seemed to be racking his brains for the explanation of this mystery, which intrigued him intensely.

'Listen,' I said to him in a serious tone, 'you seem like a smart boy; I'm going to tell you who I am. M. Kerguen has taken me into service as his valet and brought me here with him. You know that the master sometimes has ideas that are a little … strange.'

'You don't say!' he replied in a mocking tone, and burst into laughter.

'Well, guess what? He's forbidden me to leave the garden. Why, I don't know. It's probably just a whim. But I need to go to the village. Do you want to run an errand for me?'

I slipped a coin into his hand, which caused his eye to widen.

'You have Jean-Marie's word!' he said enthusiastically. 'I'll do whatever you ask.'

'Here, do you see this letter? You have to take it to the post office without anyone seeing you.'

His reaction was a pantomime, expressing his great astonishment. No doubt he considered the task to be trivial in comparison with the princely sum he was getting in advance.

'That's not all. You must promise not to tell anyone in the village that I am here.'

He nodded enthusiastically in agreement.

'You must come back here every day to this exact place, for more errands.'

'Oh, I will,' he said with a knowing air. 'Don't worry, I'll be on time.'

'If I'm happy with you, I'll let you fish for trout in the master's pond without telling him, plus which I'll give you a piece of silver like this every week. But if you betray me, beware! I'll tell the master everything.'

He smiled triumphantly.

'On my word, I'll never betray you and you can always count on me. But,' he added after a moment's reflection, 'it won't always be me that comes. My mother sometimes sends me out to guard our black cow on the hill over there, and it's too far from the pasture for me to come over. And Blackie's cunning: if she knew I was here, she'd be off chewing old Le Goalou's cabbages, like she did once. But on those days I'll send little Rose, my twin sister. She'll run your errands, have no fear, and she won't tell anyone. We're as like as two peas: you'll recognise her easily.'

I gave him my letter (the one dated the 22nd). He tucked it in his belt, then wrapped the trout he had caught in a large handkerchief.

'Oh!' he murmured, looking at his haul. 'Old Ruk will have a good share today.'

'Who is old Ruk?'

'He's our neighbour. He's old and unwell. When the fishing is good, we share and he gets half.'

I admired the boy's frankness; he considered his daily haul from the fish-pond as a legitimate right.

'But,' he added, shaking his blond locks, 'in the winter there's nothing but fishing. Fish, fish, nothing but fish. In the summer it's different: there's fruit! Look over there in the corner at that big tree twisted against the wall. It's a pear *espalier* – and what pears!'

His eyes gleamed with pleasure as he pronounced the words.

'And how do you gather them?'

'With a long pointed pole. They fall to the ground and then I collect them.'

'So you never go into the garden?'

'Oh, never. By day there's the old gardener who hates me and who told me he'd tear my ears off if he caught me. And at night, there's Jacquot!'

There was a tremor in the child's voice as he pronounced the last words.

'Ah, yes, the bear. Is he vicious?

'Is he vicious? May Jesus help me!' exclaimed Jean-Marie. 'They release him every night the master is here and he roams the garden growling. Sometimes you can hear him from the village. One night, old Ruk's dog jumped into the garden to take a run at him – and old Ruk's dog was as big as a calf. Well, Jacquot waited for him and ate him; he would eat me too!'

'Has M. Kerguen had this nasty animal a long time?'

'A long time? I think so. Jacquot is old now. My mother has often told me the story. Ten years ago, at the festival of Loc-ahr, a big fat man came, bringing Jacquot and making him perform tricks in the village square. It seems the master saw the man and wanted to buy his bear, you understand? He asked him to come up to the house with Jacquot. The man came back down without the bear, but he showed everybody a lot of gold pieces he got from the master. He said he was very pleased to get rid of it because it cost too much to feed, and he would now be able to live in his old age. But they say the bear wasn't as ferocious in those days. It's the master that's made it mean, on purpose. He beats it and doesn't give it enough to eat.'

'But then why does Jacquot seem to like M. Kerguen?'

'Oh, there's no fear he'll touch the master, or the old gardener either. They have a secret. They grab him by the neck near the ear, somehow, like this—.'

The child suddenly interrupted what he was saying, stuffed the fish under his arm, and vanished behind the wall.

The hasty departure was caused by the sight of the old gardener appearing at the end of the garden.

I made a point of looking disinterestedly at the fish playing in the pond and the old idiot passed close to me without suspecting anything.

A great load had been taken off my mind and I was confident I would henceforth be able to communicate with the outside world without my master knowing.

3

Kerguen, Thursday

I don't know whether I shall have the strength to finish this letter. I am exhausted, devoured by fever. But, despite my extreme weakness, the events which I am about to describe are too important for me to delay writing to you.

It's not just the desire to assuage your curiosity that obliges me to write. These letters will serve as evidence, should I die during my mission.

Thus, should three days elapse without any news from me, take my letters immediately to the examining magistrate and tell him all you have learnt thus far and all that you might have guessed.

But I urgently need to describe the events of last night. Excuse the disjointed nature of my letter: my pen is trembling in my hands; I can hardly connect two thoughts together; my brain is on fire, and I need to take a moment's rest after each sentence I write.

I was already not feeling well last night: the fever was burning me up so I could hardly put my head to the pillow without experiencing intolerable pain.

I got up and opened the window: a glacial wind hit me full in the face; I felt a great relief.

I leant on the window sill and fell into a semi-trance during which I had a frightful nightmare; it seemed as though someone was pounding my head with a hammer.

How long did it last? I don't know, but I was awakened from my painful reverie by a strange noise that appeared to come from one of the rooms on the left corner of the house.

It must have been the fever that increased the sharpness of my hearing.

It sounded like a murmur: two voices speaking excitedly; one dominating the other in the silence of the night.

I opened my door carefully and took a few steps into the corridor.

I'd been right: the room in the corner of the house to my right was occupied; there was a thin strip of light under the door.

I went forward on tiptoe, hoping to catch a few words of the nocturnal conversation. I put my eye to the keyhole, but the key was in the lock and I could not distinguish the voices.

There was a silence.

It was broken after a few seconds by a voice I recognised as M. Bréhat-Kerguen's.

'I'm telling you again,' he said rapidly and in a firm voice, 'I repeat, you cannot stay here. For what reason? That's none of your business and I'm not going to tell you. But you absolutely must leave tomorrow night. I'll rent you a room in Rennes and you will go there and wait for me. After that, we'll go to England together.'

'You want me to die!' sobbed the other voice which, to my surprise, was a woman's. 'I can't possibly travel, as ill as I am.'

'Ill or not, you have to go, do you hear?' replied the other harshly. 'You must. You know I don't joke, and when I want something, it has to be so.'

'Wait a week. In a week, either I'll be dead and you'll be rid of me, or I'll be cured and I can come with you.'

'Good Lord! If I could wait a week, I wouldn't be forcing you to leave tomorrow. But in a week we have to be far away. I've already been found out in Paris. I carried out a few jobs there which attracted the attention of the police. I'm not worried about being caught. I just need the time to collect the loot and disappear. You cannot stay here, do you understand? I don't have to tell you why, but you can't. You have to hide, and hide quickly, otherwise you know what will happen to you. Your situation is no better than mine.'

'You're just trying to frighten me. How can the police discover you here? You told me they took someone else in your place.'

'Yes, but the mistake may not last long. I'm afraid of having a top detective come after me, and my philosophy is to disappear at the first sign of trouble. That's my last word: leave tomorrow during the night and let me drive you to Rennes. Otherwise, if you refuse to obey me, you know I'll get rid of you.'

'You blackguard! You would dare to kill me after all I've done for you?'

'For me? Do you think I owe you anything? It seems to me you've done very well for yourself, without taking too many risks. As for me—.'

There followed a silence, during which I could hear M. Bréhat-Kerguen pacing briskly up and down.

He stopped suddenly.

'Well? Have you decided?'

'I'm tired of always obeying you. Kill me. I'm suffering; I can't move a muscle. How can I follow you? Kill me, I'd prefer it. Since you're going to be caught one day, I'd rather die here than on the guillotine.'

'I'm going to be caught?' replied the other, sarcastically. 'Haha. I can get out of any trap. I might be caught if you stay here—and you'll be caught with me. But, if you obey me, in one week--—the time to claim the lion's share of the inheritance—I'll come and find you in Rennes and we'll go to England together. And even the Devil won't be able to find us there!'

I sensed that the argument was almost at an end, so I went cautiously back to my room and went to bed, having taken the precaution of wrapping my head in a thick scarf.

And indeed, five minutes later I heard M. Bréhat-Kerguen's heavy footsteps echoing in the corridor. He opened my door softly and played the light of his lantern on my face.

Then he left without making a noise.

4

I waited several minutes so as to be sure he had gone back to his apartment and wouldn't return.

Then I got up, even though my fever had worsened and I was suffering atrociously. I was beginning to discern the end of this murky story and, so close to solving it all, was prepared to make a superhuman effort not to succumb to my illness.

I made my way down the corridor, bent in two like an old man and leaning against the walls for support.

My limbs were shaking from the cold, yet my head was burning like a hot coal.

I eventually reached the door I was seeking, and knocked twice on the solid panels.

There was no response; pressing my ear against the keyhole, I thought I heard uneven and wheezy breathing coming from inside the room.

I knocked again. There was a deep sigh…then nothing.

Meanwhile, I felt myself getting weaker. I clutched the door mouldings with my fingers to stop myself falling down.

In my fever, I imagined the killer's footsteps echoing in the dark corridors, and was sure he would surprise me before I discovered his secret.

The secret was there, inside the room I was unable to enter! Once across the threshold, I would make the accomplice confess and so finally learn the whole story.

"Maybe," I said to myself, "if I make one supreme effort I can break down this door that looms before me like an immovable object. But the noise would attract the killer's attention and I would expire just as I was about to learn everything."

I felt the delirium invade my brain, my ideas fade away, and a cold sweat appear on my forehead.

What a horrible moment! If ever I survive such torment, I shall never forget that hour of anguish.

Finding a way into that room had become an obsession. But how?

I leant against the door frame and, with my head in my hands, I forced myself to think things through, which calmed me down. I went back to my room and collected a lamp and a pocket-knife to help me force the lock of the door to the mysterious accomplice's room. Then, I went back down the same corridor and stopped in front of the door.

I realised straight away that the door had been double-locked and thus impossible to open from the outside. I couldn't even remove the screws that secured the old oak door: they were on the inside.

A painful discouragement seized me. One hand against the damp wall of the corridor, I proceeded, head down, towards my room, eventually reaching it and locking myself in.

I threw myself fully clothed on the bed. But my state of over-excitement prevented me from benefitting from the rest I so desperately needed. I couldn't help thinking about that room, only a few metres from mine, where she who possessed the secrets I was burning to learn lay dying.

The words exchanged between the unknown woman and Bréhat-Kerguen were indelibly engraved in my memory. I ran through them slowly, thinking about every word. But the conversation was too incomplete for me to find what I wanted. Nevertheless, that brief conversation had left me convinced of one thing. Bréhat-Kerguen was a villain whose recent fratricide was by no means his first crime; moreover, he had an accomplice that he wished to get rid of at any price....And here a terrible thought struck me:

"He had insisted," I told myself, "that she leave the residence immediately. She had refused. Would he stop at a crime which would ensure her silence for all time? Apparently nobody knew she existed, so the crime could be committed with impunity. Good Grief! He could be preparing to kill her tonight."

He's going to kill her tonight!

Have you any idea of the anguish I suffered at the thought? In a few hours, in a few minutes maybe, the unique and precious testimony would be extinguished.

Three hours went by. Despite all my efforts, and even though I swallowed a considerable dose of opium, sleep still escaped me. I remained sprawled on my bed, which felt like fire despite the shivers that ran through my body. My eyes were wide open.

I turned my head slowly towards a large silver watch suspended over the headboard: it showed precisely two o'clock in the morning.

All of a sudden—was it a hallucination?—I thought I could hear a faint rustling noise in the corridor: I thought, "It must be a bat fluttering its wings." But no, the noise continued, and it resembled a human step.

I got up painfully, went to the door and stood there, holding my breath. Someone was walking along the corridor. Little by little, the night walker's slow shuffle came nearer. I heard it distinctly in front of the door, then it went further away.

The noise, barely perceptible, had a noticeable rhythm and regularity: Bréhat-Kerguen did not walk like that. His tread was uneven: I already told you he dragged his left leg a little. But, if it wasn't the master of the premises who was walking about at that time of night, who could it have been?

Consumed by curiosity and without thought of the danger I might be risking, I opened the door gently and went into the corridor.

To my right, where the mysterious room I had tried to enter a few hours before was situated, all was dark and quiet. I then turned to the left: here is what I saw. At the end of the narrow corridor a large black shadow detached itself from a luminous background. It advanced slowly, straight and stiff like a ghost.

I had to clear up this strange mystery at all costs. From the day I joined M. Bréhat-Kerguen's service, I had always carried a pair of pistols on me, as a precautionary measure. I loaded the pistols and went forward, muffling my steps, towards the receding shadow.

I was walking quite quickly and was soon only a few yards from the apparition. I adjusted my step so that it did not suspect my presence.

I cannot describe my emotions I felt as I started this adventure. This shadow, this ghost wandering the corridors of this old mansion, the asylum of a murderer, had a fantastic and supernatural aspect impossible to describe. Could it be one of his victims who had returned, as terrible and as implacable as remorse itself, sitting on the murderer's headboard and torturing his sleep?

The shadow was still advancing with its slow, measured steps like the movements of a clock. It had reached the end of the long corridor. I noticed, thanks to the faint light in front of it, the top steps of a small stone staircase that seemed to have been carved out of the thick wall.

I took a few steps to get closer, in order to see the direction it was going to take.

Just at that moment, ill luck would have it that I stubbed my foot against one of the corridor slabs that had been loosened through the action of time.

"I'm lost!" I said to myself in dread.

Surely enough, the night prowler turned round sharply; the light it was holding in its hand illuminated it from head to toe.

I stopped as well, both hands positioned over the butts of the pistols, ready to sell my life dearly if, as I suspected, the unknown person was one of the murderer's accomplices. Imagine my surprise when the shadow remained still and silent before me; it even seemed unaware of my presence. I took several steps forward and approached it.

I realised then that this semi-fantastic being was in fact a woman, tall of stature and with a hard, lined face; wearing a coloured madras headscarf; with long, greying locks tumbling to her shoulders; and a large grey shawl enveloping her entirely. Her complexion was as pale as death; her eyes, wide open, stared fixedly at the ceiling without movement or expression; her mouth was set in a frightening smile.

I recoiled, appalled. There was no doubt in my mind: it was *she*, the dying woman who, three hours earlier, had been involved in that mysterious conversation with Bréhat-Kerguen. She was the accomplice in his crimes; she knew all his secrets. I rushed towards her, determined to frighten her with my threats, to drag out of her willy-nilly those truths she held to her bosom. I assumed that she stayed immobile and frozen out of fear; that it would be easy to profit from her initial fright; that the sight of me would make her confess to her crimes and those of her accomplice.

But, once my face was close to hers, once I noticed the fixed expression in her eyes, the paleness of her clenched lips, the damp sweat on her temple; and when I saw the emaciated chest that the breath of life no longer appeared to animate, the truth dawned on me.

The poor woman was in the grip of a fit of somnambulism.

With her two hands, she clasped a small lamp to her bosom. Suddenly, with a brusque movement, one of her hands dropped and seized my wrist in a vice-like grip. She didn't look at me, however, her eyes were still raised upwards; how had she managed to see me? At the same time, her lips relaxed and a slight breath escaped. I thought she was about to speak and so brought my ear close to her lips; but she shut her mouth, turned abruptly and, without letting go of my hand, restarted the slow march that had been briefly interrupted.

I gathered all my courage and followed her resolutely, without trying to disengage my arm which she now held in the iron grip that caused me so much pain.

She moved towards the narrow staircase where, a few moments earlier, I had noticed the steps. We went down: I counted twenty-eight steps before we arrived at a landing where my strange companion stopped. She turned again towards me and uttered a few unintelligible and incoherent sounds. I guessed we had arrived at the first floor of the mansion. In front of us ran a long corridor that disappeared into the darkness of the night.

Then the somnambulist let go of my arm and put a finger to her lips as if urging silence and took the lead again. I followed, my heart beating as if to burst. Where was she taking me like this? I knew that Bréhat-Kerguen's apartment was on the same floor, and the door of his room opened on to the same corridor. What if he heard our footsteps? Suppose he came suddenly out of his room and saw me with this woman who knew the secret of his crimes? Nothing causes more anxiety than the apprehension of an anticipated danger that one senses and that could appear in one's path. At that moment I stopped breathing and stopped living; all my intelligence was concentrated on a single thought: my eyes attempted to pierce the thick shadows, my uneasy ear was listening to whether, through the deep silence of the night, any slight noise could be heard emanating from that end of the corridor which we were approaching step by step.

Suddenly the shadow I was following stopped again. She turned to me and beckoned me come close to her. I obeyed. Then she placed her emaciated hand on a wooden door distinguishable by the naïve sculptures carved into it by artists from olden times.

I didn't understand what the sign meant, nor why my mysterious guide had stopped in front of this particular door. I knew that on this side of the mansion there were empty apartments, uninhabited for a very long time, that the gardener used for storing fruit and vegetables during the winter.

My companion appeared to notice my hesitation. She murmured as she again placed he finger on the door:

'It's here. Are you afraid? He's a deep sleeper.'

Who was she talking to in her dream? Did the master use this room? I asked her in a low voice, but slowly and articulating each word.

'Does Bréhat-Kerguen sleep here?'

'Yes,' she replied.

And I saw on her tight lips the same fearful smile I had seen before.

She gently inserted a rusty key in the great iron lock, turned it without making a noise, and pushed the door wide open.

'Come on,' she said.

I followed her in and she locked the door.

The room my strange guide had led me into was of medium size with a very high ceiling; the walls were covered with tapestries that time and humidity had damaged. The appearance of the room intrigued me enormously. Obviously it was inhabited. To the rear was a four-poster bed with a canopy, whose curtains were drawn. Near the bed was a high-backed armchair on which a man's clothes had been negligently thrown. A little farther away, against the window from which a small shaving mirror had been suspended, a washbasin supported a bowl full of soapy water; an otter-skin cap and a hunting whip had been thrown on the pedestal table in the middle of the room. Above the tall fireplace, where two blackened logs lay in a thick pile of ashes, lay a double-barrelled shotgun and a flintlock pistol. Finally, on a bedside table stood a brass candlestick with a half-used candle and, alongside, a folded newspaper.

Without hesitation, the somnambulist walked towards the bed, lamp in hand. I recoiled instinctively and remained in the dark. An inexpressible anguish had gripped me and I trembled with emotion and—I'm not afraid to say so—fear. Yes, the thought that this man—who must have the light sleep of the assassin—was going to wake up at any moment and find himself facing this unfortunate woman; at the thought of the awful scene that was probably going to be enacted before my eyes, I found myself seized with a harrowing dread. Nevertheless, I resolved to stay. Curiosity triumphed over emotion and I wished to be present, as an invisible witness, at this nocturnal meeting of two criminals. I hoped to hear from their own mouths the terrible revelations that should provide the denouement to my dangerous adventures.

She approached the bed and tugged gently at the curtains, whose rings squeaked on the rusty rails, then bent over the pillow to listen.

Motivated by ill-considered curiosity, I peered out at that side and recoiled in shock. The bed was empty! The sheets and covers were crumpled in disorder, the pillow thrown against the wall.

I stood by the side of my mysterious companion who remained immobile, leaning over the imaginary sleeper. I noted with astonishment that the sheets were full of holes and tears; it appeared that over the years they had served as a pasture for legions of mice.

The woman stood up slowly and whispered in my ear:

'He's sound asleep. The concoction we gave him worked well.'

Then she seized my hand and, indicating the large space under the bed, said:

'Hide there and let's do it quickly.'

The truth, the awful truth, started to dawn on me. I did what she told me: I lay down by the side of the bed. She took the lamp that she had left on the bedside table, hid it under her copious shawl, and hid in one of the dark corners of the room.

A few moments later, I went to join her and said:

'It's done!'

'Already?' she replied, letting out a deep sigh.

She went back once more to the bed, ran her emaciated hand over the covers and, placing it on the spot where she supposed the sleeper's chest to be, waited anxiously.

'Yes,' she said eventually, in a cavernous voice. 'He's dead. It's effective, better than a knifing, isn't it?'

The words came out of her mouth erratically and breathlessly. The unfortunate woman seemed to be bearing a great burden. A shiver ran through her whole body.

At last, she gripped my arm in her two hands and said:

'Now, we have to get rid of him. You will take his place, I shall be your wife, and I shall be rich!'

At that moment my eye fell on the newspaper lying on the bedside table. I disengaged myself gently from the woman's grip and brought the paper up to the lamp. It bore the date 25 January 1836. It was now January 1846.

I understood everything. The mysterious scene, in which I had just played a part, was a repetition of the drama that had been acted out ten years before, day for day, in this very room, next to this very bed.

M. Bréhat-Kerguen had been dead for ten years, killed by an audacious bandit who had dared to take his name, his fortune, and even his likeness.

This woman had been his accomplice in crime and had become the wife of the murderer.

Do you remember, during the autopsy on the unfortunate banker of Rue Cassette, the steward, M. Prosper, had told us that M. Bréhat-Kerguen had married his servant?

I found out later that her name was Yvonne.

5

Locnevinen, Auberge de l'Ecu de France

Friday, eleven o'clock at night

I was obliged to interrupt my last letter, already very long. The events of Wednesday night had already tired me beyond endurance. I almost didn't have the strength to drag myself to the garden wall to give my letter to Jean-Marie.

I'm delighted with my little messenger; he seems very intelligent and very discreet. I gave him a note for the postmaster in which I asked for him to be given any letters addressed to me. In any case, I doubt that I shall be staying here long. I'm almost at the end of my task and, dead or alive, you will see me soon.

But I need to take up my story where I left off.

The somnambulist, after the re-enactment of the crime, dragged me rapidly from the room and double-locked it.

She walked rapidly now, so fast that I had difficulty keeping up. She climbed the narrow staircase cut into the wall and when she reached the top step she stopped suddenly and, pressing herself against me, murmured in a strangled voice:

'Do you hear me? Do you hear me? They are after us. They have seen us. We're lost.'

Then she continued on her way, bent double, shivering and hollow-eyed. I followed her to her room, where she locked us in. There was an expression of sheer terror on her ashen face. She eventually got into bed, closed her eyes, pulled the bedcovers up to her mouth, and chewed on them violently.

I stood for a while by her bed, studying her carefully. Soon her breathing became calmer and her face less pale; I realised she had fallen into a natural sleep.

I let a few minutes go by and then, putting my hand on her shoulder, I shook her aggressively to wake her up. She opened her eyes and sat up immediately. Seeing me next to her, she made a fearful gesture. I thought she was going to cry out; I quickly put my hand on her mouth and said firmly:

'Don't talk. Don't cry for help. It would be useless. I am now the master of your life.'

'Who are you?' she asked in a despairing voice, staring at me wild-eyed.

'I am your judge.'

She shivered violently.

'I know your past,' I continued in a stern voice, 'and I know your crime. I know that during the night of January 25th 1836, you killed your master.'

'No! No! It wasn't me!' she cried, struggling. 'It was *him*!'

'Yes, I know you weren't alone in the room with M. Bréhat-Kerguen, I know you had an accomplice. You must give me the name of that accomplice.'

She passed her bony hand across her sweat-soaked brow.

'His name,' she murmured in a faint voice. 'Wait, I'm trying to remember. His name is—.'

She didn't complete the sentence. Her two arms straightened convulsively, and she fell back heavily against the pillow, her head thrown back. I thought she was dead: indeed, there was no breath in her chest, and her hands and neck were cold. However, by placing my ear on her heart I could detect a very faint beat. I decided that the poor woman was in the grip of that terrible nervous condition known as catalepsy.

I stepped back and prepared to leave the room. What need did I have, after all, to know the name of the killer? Hadn't I already guessed it? Didn't I know that there was only one man in the world capable of committing such a labyrinth of crimes with such skill and audacity?

I was about to leave and go back to my room, when I thought I heard a familiar uneven tread in the corridor: the kind that belonged to sailors or convicts.

It was him! He was coming to kill his victim.

Flight was impossible. I looked around to find a place to hide.

Finally I hid myself behind one of the long window curtains. They were very thick, no doubt to prevent the light from the room being visible from the garden. It was by concealing myself thus, you will remember, that led to me discovering Dr. Wickson's ruse.

I was just in time. The curtain had scarcely fallen back into place when the key squeaked in the lock and the door opened slowly.

The killer seemed very agitated. His face was pale, and his brow furrowed. The grey wig perched askew on his head let a jet black lock of hair escape.

He approached the bed with hesitant steps and, lifting the small lantern he held in his hand, he looked attentively at the face of the old woman.

His brow cleared suddenly and he breathed a sigh of relief. He obviously believed her dead, and the death saved him from another crime.

He took hold of her icy hand, lifted it, and let it fall. He placed his ear on her marble chest.

Then he straightened up slowly, considered his accomplice again with a strange smile, and left the room as quietly as he had come.

As he turned, I distinctly saw a long needle stuck in the cuff of his dressing-gown, shining in the light of the lantern.

6

The next day my terrible master wanted me to serve him lunch. Although I was exhausted by the emotions of the previous night, I obeyed, for fear of arousing his suspicions.

During the meal, he examined me furtively and frequently; his piercing look seemed to probe the secrets of my soul.

Just as he was about to leave the table, someone knocked at the door.

I went to open it. It was the old gardener, Yves, who brought a letter addressed to M. Bréhat-Kerguen. I looked at the envelope: the letter came from Rennes.

My master unsealed it eagerly. As he did so, I passed behind him. I noticed at the foot of the letter a large signature with a complicated flourish that I assumed was that of a lawyer.

He read the epistle twice with great care, then rose slowly and headed for the door.

As he drew level with me, he appeared somewhat undecided. He seemed about to speak, but obviously decided that it would be best to guard his silence, for he turned his back on me abruptly and left.

That was when I dragged myself out to the garden wall to hand to Jean-Marie the letter that I wrote to you this morning.

As I was returning from that expedition, which had taken more than half an hour and drained me of all my remaining reserves, I noticed the old gardener, who was looking at Jacquot the bear with a melancholy eye.

I went up to him quietly. He did not hear me coming.

'Poor creature,' he murmured, holding the ferocious animal by a small gold ring attached to his velvety ear, 'you're going to be really unhappy for three days. The master has forbidden me to give you anything to eat until he returns.'

'What?' I said, placing my hand on the good fellow's shoulder. 'Has M. Bréhat-Kerguen gone away?'

The old fool gave a great shout.

'Jesus my saviour!' he cried, shaking off my hand. 'The master told me not to tell you. Or it's the stick! The stick!'

And he ran away, raising one arm to the sky and holding the other to his shoulder, as if he could feel in advance the terrible punishment he had been promised.

The truth came to me with perfect clarity. The letter received that morning summoned my master to appear without further delay in Rennes, to settle the matter of the succession.

He had left hurriedly, while I was not watching. He had forbidden anyone to speak to me during his absence for fear that, finding myself free to act, I would continue my investigations and violate his order not to leave the grounds.

His marvellous perspicacity had revealed to him who I was, I could no longer doubt that.

So why did he treat me so carefully? Why did he hesitate to get rid of me, he who would not have hesitated to kill the unfortunate woman he had made his wife, were it not that her apparent death had rendered that crime pointless?

That's what I can't work out.

A deep growl from Jacquot interrupted my thoughts.

The bear was walking up and down in its cage, its muzzle close to the ground and its hair on end, growling with a famished air.

I remembered what the old gardener had just told me unintentionally. The master had forbidden anyone to feed Jacquot until his return.

Was it only on his return that he would prepare him the sort of meal he desired? I was unhappy with that thought and vowed not to leave Jacquot hungry for so long.

The bear had reared up on its hind legs and was shaking its great head and looking at me through little eyes that had nothing tender in them.

I took a few steps towards its cage.

The movement of the head increased. It put its paws through the bars as if it wanted to give me an unforgettable welcome.

The gold ring in its ear was within reach of my hand.

I seized it and put my finger through the ring, just as the gardener had done a few moments before.

The bear's ferocity disappeared straight away.

He closed his eyes with a fatherly look, dropped down heavily on his paws, and lay down at my feet.

I knew how to tame Jacquot, already an important point in my favour.

The master's absence left me at least three days of liberty. I had more than enough time to carry out the searches I had planned to do.

But I was so feeble at that moment that I decided to postpone everything to the following day.

It was as much as I could do to climb the two flights of stairs and throw myself on the bed.

I didn't even have the strength to go as far as the sick woman's room to make sure that her cataleptic sleep had not given way to death itself.

It was then three o'clock in the afternoon.

I slept soundly and only awakened at five o'clock the next morning.

My fever had receded and my mind was very clear; I felt an extraordinary vigour in all my limbs. I think the belief that I would soon have the complete solution to the mystery helped my recovery enormously.

I waited impatiently for daybreak. As soon as the first cold, pale rays of the winter sun penetrated the window panes brilliant with frost, I got up and dressed rapidly.

My first task was to visit the room where the bandit's accomplice lay. Still the same icy calm appearance, the same silence, the same impassiveness.

Then I left the room and went out into the courtyard.

7

Jacquot was already up and making the quite natural complaints of a bear that had gone to bed the night before without supper. I went inside to find a large side of meat and threw it to him. He thanked me with a howl of joy and set about devouring it with relish.

I had resolved to get into the killer's apartment, where I hoped to find incriminating evidence: material proof without which the police will seldom proceed.

Entering by the door was out of the question, because there was a secret lock and he had taken the key with him.

I wanted to try to get in through the window.

There was a tall Norwegian fir in front of the house, as I already mentioned, whose dense branches brushed the walls of the house and whose slender top reached the window of my room.

I climbed the tree without much difficulty, for the closely growing boughs and the straight branches formed a sort of ladder that was practicable enough.

Reaching the first floor, I pressed my face against the window that I presumed to be the master's bedroom. But, by bad luck, the curtains were so tightly drawn that I could not make out the interior of the room.

This setback didn't discourage me, however, and I started to think about the best way to get into the room without leaving any trace of a break-in.

While I was deep in meditation, perched in the tree like a new Robinson Crusoe, I happened to look up and noticed, to the left of the big window, a smaller one, square in shape, which seemed to provide light to a chamber adjacent to the master's room.

I climbed a little higher in the tree, until my eye was level with it and tried to peer in. But the green canopy was so thick above my head that I couldn't see anything.

I separated the branches that blocked out the light and looked again.

After a short while, and once my eyes had become accustomed to the dark, I realised that my predictions had been right. The little window illuminated a chamber of about six feet square. It even seemed I could make out a black patch on the left hand wall that marked the place of a communicating door between the chamber and the apartment.

My eye soon caught another white patch in a dark corner, of a bizarre and imprecise form. One would have guessed an enormous spider's web.

It was a skeleton.

The sight of it redoubled my enthusiasm and fed my curiosity. I wanted at all costs to get into the mysterious little room. After a few minutes of reflection, I devised a plan that would allow access without leaving any trace of my passage.

With my knife I cut one of the resinous branches—the one that appeared to be the driest—and set fire to it with my lighter. Then I held the flaming torch close to my person.

The window was comprised of four small panes set in lead frames.

I used the flame of the torch to bring the tip of my knife to white heat and applied the cutting edge to the lead.

It was only after several fruitless attempts that I finally saw the lead frame fall on to the window sill.

I picked up the glass pane carefully and deposited in on the window sill.

I had completed the work with the skill of an accomplished burglar. I passed my hand through the opening and worked the rusty bolt that locked the frame.

The window opened, and a penetrating odour, like that of a funeral cave, assailed my nostrils.

I picked up my resin torch and, sliding in through the narrow space, found myself in a chamber slightly longer than it was wide and whose bare walls were oozing dampness.

I went first to the skeleton that had attracted my attention.

It was that of a tall, well-built man. I examined it carefully and was struck by the singular shape of the two feet. They were very long and the deformed upper bone formed a protuberance that had no doubt been painful.

You will recall that I made the same observation on the day of the autopsy, when I lifted the shroud covering M. Bréhat-Lenoir's feet.

It was a striking coincidence. I measured the height of the skeleton precisely, then continued my investigations.

I didn't detect even the slightest gap in the walls to indicate any kind of secret hiding place.

They had been coated with a hard cement that provided a perfectly smooth surface.

As I was examining the walls of the damp chamber, my foot struck an obstacle. I lowered my torch and saw that one of the red tiles on the floor of the chamber had been slightly lifted by the tip of my foot. I knelt down and lifted it up quite easily with my long fingers.

A very deep and narrow hole had been created in that spot and I pulled out a long, thin leather bag, tied shut by a drawstring.

I found several objects in the bag. I shall enumerate then in detail. This simple list will give you some idea of the importance of my discovery:

1. A set of dissecting instruments made in England. As far as I could tell, bearing in mind my inexperience, they were very well made.

2. A red leather case, round in shape, containing five very fine and very solid needles whose points were stained with brown. The lower part of the case could be separated. I found a small crystal flask there, full of a thick brown fluid. I put the case carefully in my pocket.

3. Five silver dinner place settings, with the monogram C.B under a count's crown.

4. A superb diamond ring.

5. A gold watch with an elaborate monogram under a knight's helmet.

I didn't find any other jewellery. The killer had undoubtedly brought back those pieces he could not have sold in Paris without running a risk, and he was probably counting on getting rid of them in England.

I had been luckier in my search than I had dared to hope. This last discovery provided me with the thread that would surely lead me through the labyrinth of crimes. And, even if I didn't yet know all the tortuous avenues, I at least knew the starting point and could make out the various stages of the route.

It was strange: I had just reached the end I so ardently desired, and yet the unexpectedly fruitful results of my searches and observations left me almost cold and indifferent.

It seemed to me, in my hour of triumph, that the deductions that had led me to the goal had come to mind naturally and without effort, and I could put behind me the memories of the frightening work, and the hours of insomnia and suffering, that this relentless pursuit of the truth had cost me.

8

Today, Jean-Marie brought me the letter in which you informed me that Dr. Wickson had left the capital and that there was no more talk of nocturnal attacks in your good city of Paris.

That doesn't surprise me: you know why.

I thank you sincerely for the expressions of friendship you have given me and your concern for my health.

Alas! As I have told you, the energy that drives me is all on the surface and once the task to which I have dedicated myself is accomplished, I shall once again succumb under the weight of so much fatigue.

Thus the hunting hound expires on the body of the stag it has been chasing.

This letter will doubtless be one of the last I write. I await the master this evening; the trap is set for tonight, and once he is delivered into the hands of justice, I shall leave for Paris.

I shall now pick up my story where I left off last night.

After my search was finished, I came down from the tree with the needle case in my pocket, and returned to my room. I scratched the point of one of the needles which were, as you know, coated with a brown substance that scraped off as a powder; then I emptied the crystal flask that contained the awful fluid and washed it thoroughly.

This done, I took some soot and mixed it with water, substituting the anodyne liquid for the subtle poison the flask had contained. I also coated the points of the needles with it.

Then I went back down and returned to the funeral cave by the same perilous route.

I placed all the objects back into the leather bag and put the bag back in the hiding place, then adjusted the small tile that hid the opening.

I used my knife, heated by the flame, to reseal the glass pane in its lead frame, and, once this lengthy procedure was over, descended through the fir's densely packed branches.

It was half past twelve, the time of my regular rendezvous with Jean-Marie.

I found my little Breton out of sorts. The pond had frozen over and he was throwing large stones to break the ice that was depriving him of his daily prey.

'Good day, Monsieur Pierre,' he cried in his silvery voice. 'You're not sick any more.'

'No, my boy, thank you. I'm feeling much better. Well, the fish aren't biting today?'

'It's a real shame,' he said, disappointedly, running his hand through his thick blond hair. 'The ice is harder than the stones. Here, look, they slide on the surface without breaking it. Old Ruk is sick, and if I don't bring him anything, he might die, the poor man.'

I gave him one piece of silver for old Ruk and another for himself. This extravagance of a nabob brought forth an exclamation of surprise, and his eyes sparkled with joy.

I gave him my letter, urging him once more to use great caution.

Then I asked him:

'Do you know how far it is from here to Locnevin?'

Locnevin is the county seat.

The child thought for a moment.

'Upon my word, I've never been there. But I heard it was a good two and a half leagues, nearly three.'

'Do you know anybody from these parts that could take me there?'

'What? You want to leave the manor house?'

'Yes. The master has given me two days of rest, and I would like to see the town.'

'Do you want to leave straight away?'

'Yes.'

'Wait. The wheelwright has a cabriolet and a good horse. He's the one who takes M. Kerguen whenever he goes on an errand. But the wheelwright left at noon yesterday to go into town and hasn't come back. Ah! There's old Claude who has a horse for his mill, but he hasn't got a carriage.'

'No matter, I'll take the horse by itself.'

'I can go and ask him, if you want.'

'No, I'll come with you. Does he live far away?'

'About half an hour from here. On the edge of town.'

'That's fine. Wait for me at the end of that row of chestnut trees; I'll meet you in ten minutes.'

The trip across the rugged and bracing Breton countryside, coupled with the gentle chattering of my guide, dissipated the last remaining traces of the illness that had overwhelmed me the night before.

Old Claude gave me no trouble about renting his horse for two days. His mill was not working because the river was frozen, and I suspect he was not displeased that I would be providing nourishment for his animal for twenty-four hours.

I obtained the information I needed as to the best route and the best hotel in town and, thanks to the sturdy legs of my horse, took less than three hours to reach the Auberge de L'Ecu de France, situated on the main square of Locnevin.

I ordered lunch right away, for I had not eaten all morning; then I asked the innkeeper to tell me the whereabouts of the county court.

My host indicated a monumental building on the square whose walls had been blackened by time.

'It's over there,' he said. 'You'll see a two-handed sword outside, the kind they used for cutting off heads before the guillotine was invented.'

I thanked the innkeeper for the historical insight and, on arriving in the court, asked to see the examining magistrate.

M. Donneau, examining magistrate of the court of Locnevin, is a young man of no more than thirty years of age. The lively gleam in his eye reveals his energy and intelligence; his manner is very courteous. One can see straight away that he brings to his difficult profession as much finesse as decisiveness.

'Monsieur,' I said without preamble, 'you have doubtless heard speak, some ten years ago, of a series of audacious crimes committed in Paris by a gang led by a certain Red Bomber.'

'Certainly, monsieur,' replied the young magistrate, who seemed somewhat surprised by my question. 'The affair was very celebrated back then and I was better placed than anyone to know the details, because my father presided over the hearings.'

He told me his name and I remembered that the magistrate in charge when I argued my first case was indeed a M. Donneau.

'So, monsieur,' I continued, 'given your knowledge of the affair, you must know that the man who led the brigands with such skill escaped the clutches of the police.'

'Yes, indeed. It was even thought that he had been killed by his own gang.'

'Well, monsieur, I am here to inform you that the man is still alive and to offer to place him in your hands.'

The examining magistrate looked at me in astonishment.

I started to tell the story you know only too well, from the visit of M. Bienassis on January 3 to Louis Guérin's room, to the search I conducted in the killer's secret cave.

While I was talking, the magistrate looked at me with the air of naïve astonishment that can be seen on the faces of children when their grandmother tells them of the marvellous events of a fairy tale.

9

When I had finished painting the dark and sinister picture of my fight against this man, M. Donneau gripped my hand firmly and told me of the profound interest my strange odyssey had aroused.

The young magistrate could not conceal the joy he felt, at the beginning of his career, to be undertaking what promised to be a successful prosecution of such a celebrated and redoubtable criminal.

He could foresee the sensation this affair would cause and could already savour the glory that would inevitably be reflected on his name.

'And you're certain that he will return tomorrow?'

'That's precisely the time to travel to Rennes and back, and I doubt that he'll dawdle on the way.'

'You know better than I his habits and the layout of the premises. What is the best way to capture him without meeting any resistance?'

I explained in a few words the methods I had settled on after careful consideration, which seemed to me to be the quickest and safest.

He approved of them wholeheartedly and told me he would personally lead an enterprise of such importance.

He led me out with many handshakes and congratulations—the kind one gives to someone to whom one is about to owe one's fortune.

As I was leaving the magistrate's chambers, it struck six on the ancient town clock.

The night was so dark that one could scarcely distinguish the sagging doors and twisted roofs of the old houses. I decided it was more prudent not to return to Kerguen that night. The roads were bad and I was fearful that I might get lost in the pitch darkness and fall into a pothole.

So I returned to the Auberge de l'Ecu de France and took dinner there, not forgetting to ask that old Claude's horse be well taken care of. Then I shut myself in my room in order to write to you.

I eventually went to bed, for I was exhausted, but my sleep was fitful.

At eight o'clock in the morning I was going, as fast as my little horse's legs could carry me, from Locnevin to Kerguen.

On the outskirts of the town, I met Jean-Marie who shouted for joy when he saw me and held up his little sister who was with him, telling her to bid me a good day.

I got down from the horse and took the boy to one side.

'You are going to ride the nag with me as far as the mansion,' I told him, 'and after that you can take it back to old Claude.'

He agreed and sat with me in the saddle. On the way, I told him:

'Jean-Marie, I'm going to be leaving here soon. You've shown a lot of enthusiasm and intelligence in the errands you've run for me so, before I go, I want you to have a souvenir. But you need to do one more thing for me. Listen carefully and remember exactly what I say. From nine o'clock tonight until midnight, you must stand by at the ready on the hill they call La Lavandière; you must bring a cowherd's horn with you and, when you see a light in the window above the big fir tree, you must blow the horn several times as loudly as you can.'

The child turned in the saddle and looked at me with eyes and mouth wide open.

'You know I demand the utmost discretion. Now promise me to do what I ask and not tell anyone at all.'

'Ah! Bless me, that's a strange idea you've got there. But I said I'd do anything you asked, so you can count on me. I'll borrow Eudes Riou's big horn that you can hear a league away on a clear day; I'll slip in through the stable window and get to the hill; from there I'll be able to see the side of the house. Don't worry, I've got good eyes and I'll be able to see the light.'

We had arrived at the row of chestnut trees.

I jumped off the horse and lifted Jean-Marie down.

'Now,' I told him, 'give this piece to old Claude for the use of his horse and keep the other for yourself. If you do everything I just told you well, you'll get ten more pieces of silver just like that.'

I left the dumbfounded child thanking me profusely and pledging loyalty, and went in to the mansion.

10

Locnevin, Sunday

COUNTY COURT OF LOCNEVIN
Examining Magistrate's Chambers

Last night there was a terrible storm. There was an extremely violent wind and snowflakes, driven by the storm, came in through the window and landed on my face.

It was seven o'clock at night when I set up my observation post.

My eyes gradually adjusted to the darkness and I could distinguish, through the curtain of snow and the shadows, the iron gate of the garden.

Jacquot was wandering around outside the house howling ominously. Luckily I had been able to steal a sizeable piece of meat from the larder, and had thrown it to him to calm him down.

Time went by slowly. Each minute felt like a century. A feeling of dread started to come over me.

I went over the plan for capturing the bandit in my mind. I found it riddled with problems. I feared we would have to abort everything and the killer would escape justice once again.

Suppose he wasn't coming back? Suppose his trip was nothing but a ruse to throw his pursuers off the scent?...

Perhaps, instead of taking the road to Rennes, he had taken the road to Brest. Perhaps, while I was waiting here to seize him in his lair, he was already on a boat taking him across the ocean.

All these thoughts crowded my mind and made the hours of wait even harder to bear.

The clock struck ten.

Suddenly I thought I could see, through the dark night, a feeble light wavering as it advanced slowly, leaving a luminous trail on the garden snow.

I leaned out of the window to try to get a closer look; the light had disappeared.

"It was a hallucination," I said to myself.

And I let a deep sigh of discouragement.

But my eyes had not left the spot where the light had disappeared.

It seemed to me that the darkness was more intense there. I could make out a dark patch on the snow.

Then the patch seemed to split into two.

"He has an accomplice," I told myself. "All is lost."

A long growl reached my ears and reassured me.

The accomplice was Jacquot, who had just greeted his master.

And, shortly afterwards, I saw the dark lantern on the move again.

It reached the courtyard door and went to the corner where the bear's cage was situated.

"He's going to check that his instructions have been obeyed," I thought, "and that Jacquot really is starving after three days."

Eventually the light advanced again, with the same deliberate speed towards the residence, and I heard the front door close with a barely perceptible noise.

It was then that I took the lamp that I had hidden behind the curtains of my bed, extended my arm out of the window, and raised it three times.

I waited several minutes. My heart was beating strongly enough to burst my chest.

"If only Jean-Marie is at his post," I thought to myself as I started to signal a second time.

A plaintive bellow could be heard despite the storm, coming from La Lavandière hill.

The same deep, prolonged sound was heard four more times.

Then, from my high vantage post, I saw a red rocket trace a luminous path in the air from a spot about a league away. It was the signal I had agreed with the examining magistrate, who had been waiting for the right moment in one of the inns of Loc-ahr.

I closed the window and extinguished the lamp.

Now I needed to verify that it was indeed the bandit who had returned home.

I therefore left my room and, following the wall closely, I went to see whether I could hear anything in his apartment.

At the moment when, arriving at the end of the corridor, I put my foot on the staircase, the noise of a door closing could be heard on the first floor, and at the same time a slow and uneven tread reverberated in the silence of the night.

Luckily I had taken the precaution of removing my shoes and was able to get back to my room without making a noise.

I slipped into my bed, pulled the covers up to my chin, and pretended to be asleep. After about a minute, the nocturnal stroller passed in front of my bedroom door without stopping. He gently opened the door of his accomplice's room.

A little later, I heard him come back from visiting the "dead woman."

He quietly inserted a key in the door lock, opened the door, and came over to my bed. I sensed the light from the lantern on my closed eyelids.

He walked about in my room, apparently conducting a thorough search.

I heard the door shut and I assumed he had left; however, no matter how hard I strained to hear, I could detect no footsteps in the corridor.

There was total silence except for the gusting wind.

I stayed in bed, fearful that he may get the idea to come back.

Suddenly, I felt a hand slip under the covers, my right leg was seized as if by a vice, and at the same time I felt a sharp stab of pain in my heel.

I let out a loud cry and fainted.

11

The blackout caused by the sudden surprise, helped no doubt by the intense nervous stress of the previous two hours, saved my life.

For the killer, seeing me pale and lifeless, assumed I was dead and left the room.

When I came to, my first reaction was to run to the door and barricade it solidly.

I then inspected the slight wound I had received on the heel. There were a few drops of blood, mixed with a brown liquid that I recognised as the inoffensive mixture I had substituted for the dreaded curare.

I prepared my two pistols and put them in my pockets. I had decided that if the killer were to return I would blow his brains out, even if that were to rob M. Donneau of the glory of capturing the celebrated bandit alive.

My watch showed eleven o'clock. It was already an hour since I had given the signal. The moment was approaching when a decisive battle would take place between the killer and the man whom he thought had become his victim. I was quivering with impatience; it seemed to me that M. Donneau was taking far too long to arrive.

I opened my window with infinite caution and listened carefully to try and detect, in the teeth of the storm, the signal announcing the arrival of the magistrate and his henchmen.

A quarter of an hour went by.

At last, when the moaning of the wind started to diminish, I thought I heard a soft, prolonged whistling noise that I took at first to be the last sigh of the tempest.

But the whistle repeated itself three or more times with the same intensity. It came from the same area of the garden as the fish-pond. There was no more doubt: it was M. Donneau and his men.

I pulled one of the sheets off the bed and twisted it rapidly so as to make a rope.

I attached the improvised cable to the iron bar of my window and let myself down the wall until I could feel one of the long branches of the fir tree under my hand.

I clutched the branch while I attached the free end of the rope to it, as close as possible to the trunk. In this way, I created a suspension bridge between the fir and the window.

Then I climbed down to the base of the tree and went as quickly as possible towards the garden wall.

Halfway there, a menacing growl stopped me. It was Jacquot, who had been lying under a clump of shrubs and who, getting up as I approached, barred my way.

I tried talking softly to him to keep him quiet; but the bear was in a bad mood, having been awakened from his sleep, and he responded to my advances by rearing up on his hind legs and coming towards me, with the intention of squeezing me in his powerful embrace.

When he was at half a metre from my chest, I ran my hand quickly through the thick fur on his brow and seized the ring that pierced his ear.

The bear let out a suppressed growl of anger, dropped back on his four legs and lay down on the ground.

At that moment I felt a great debt to the killer for the marvellous way in which he had trained Jacquot.

He had become as docile as a lamb. I threaded my belt through his earring and tied it solidly to the base of a shrub.

Jacquot let out a small growl that seemed more like a sigh of resignation and stretched out at full length in the snow.

I hurried towards the garden wall. Several stones had come away from their sockets in the cement and I was able to haul myself up to the top of the wall.

'Are you there?' I asked quietly.

'Yes,' replied a voice I recognised as that of the young magistrate. 'Can we come in?'

'Come quickly. We haven't a moment to lose.'

Within a minute, the magistrate and the five *gendarmes* that accompanied him had clambered over the wall and assembled by the fish-pond.

'Good,' I announced once I saw they were all present. 'Follow me quietly and stay close to the ground.'

We followed the wall until we could see the outline of the mansion.

Then we marched straight towards the closest corner.

In that way, we could not be seen from any of the windows of the façade.

After that, we moved silently, staying close to the walls until we reached the large fir tree. We stopped there and very quietly took stock.

It was agreed that I should serve as guide to our little team, so I started to climb first, followed by the magistrate and our brave *gendarmes* who, in view of the perilous ascent, had removed their sabres and were only carrying their pistols.

We proceeded slowly and with great care.

Just as I reached the first floor, level with the killer's window, it suddenly opened!

He appeared, clad in his dressing-gown, with a scarf around his head and leant out of the window in quiet enjoyment of his pipe.

His face was barely a metre from mine. I hid behind the trunk of the tree, whose branches at that point were luckily very dense.

The storm had died down and a solemn silence had taken the place of the roaring wind.

If, at that moment, any one of us had been overcome by fatigue and let go of the branch he was clinging to, the whole venture would have been lost.

A breeze lifted one of the curtains. I saw, by the light of a candle burning on the table, several dissecting instruments and a small grey grindstone.

Dr. Wickson was preparing for some anatomical work, and I quickly surmised which two subjects had been chosen for his experiments.

When he had finished the last few puffs and calmed his spirits enough to begin his sensitive work, he banged the ashes of his pipe out on the sill and closed the window.

I started to climb again and reached my aerial bridge five minutes later. I examined the knots carefully to make sure it was strong enough to allow my six companions to cross.

'Whew!' exclaimed the magistrate, jumping into the room after me. 'We had a narrow escape there.'

The young magistrate's eyes sparkled with delight. There was something exciting and chivalrous about our quest which seemed to captivate him.

Our *gendarmes* formed a circle around us and I lit their lanterns, instructing them to hold them with the light turned inwards.

The advice was timely, for we soon heard the killer return down the corridor. He had again taken the precaution of muffling the noise of his heavy shoes.

I put my hand on the magistrate's arm. His heart was pounding, but his face still expressed the same firmness and courage.

'He's fallen into the trap,' I whispered. 'We won't even need to beard him in his den.

But the illustrious doctor walked past the door without entering and headed, still limping, towards his accomplice's room.

I rapidly removed the bar I had placed across the door and we advanced down the corridor without making a noise.

I placed my men in two rows on either side of the corridor; M. Donneau and I were at their head.

Suddenly a horrible, strident shriek rang out from the "dead woman's" room, followed by the noise of rapid footsteps, and we saw the killer fleeing wide-eyed, his arms extended in front of him and behind him, her chest ripped open and covered in blood, a tall woman I had no difficulty in recognising.

'Stop!' cried M. Donneau in a loud voice.

Red Bomber, stunned, stopped in his tracks.

We had directed our lanterns towards him and he was caught in a circle of light.

Nevertheless, he had quickly recovered from the emotion caused by the resurrection of Yvonne. He folded his arms and there was no sign of fear in his eyes.

He seemed to be considering whether he could break through the living wall and escape through brute force.

But he obviously realised that the odds were not even. He stepped forward a few paces and, turning to me, said—with no little irony:

'Let's go. Today's the day of resurrections. I lost, policeman, and now I must pay.'

With exaggerated courtesy he extended one of his large hands. With the other, he tore off his grey wig and, drawing himself up to his full height, he looked at us calmly and proudly.

We saw a man approximately forty-five years old, of athletic build, with black curly hair and a hard, handsome face.

We handcuffed him without the slightest resistance.

The dying woman, however, dragged herself unsteadily towards him and grabbed hold of his shoulder.

'Murderer! Murderer!' she cried in her madness.

It was a truly horrible sight.

'Get rid of this woman,' muttered Red Bomber, shaking his shoulders to get away from her.

I ordered two of the *gendarmes* to take Yvonne to her bed with the utmost care.

I followed them into her room. The bed was unmade and the sheets were in disarray. A steel blade gleamed on the floor: it was a scalpel.

As soon as the invalid had been put to bed I examined her wound. The scalpel had not penetrated deeply into her chest. But the pain had been severe enough to arouse Yvonne from her cataleptic state of the last three days.

I bathed the wound and dressed it with a cold compress.

Her pulse had returned to normal. After exaltation and delirium there was now frailty and despondency.

When I rejoined the examining magistrate, he was in the process of conducting a search in the room the bandit had used for ten years.

The room, which was very spacious, was hung with dark tapestries. At the rear was a large four-poster bed on which lay a capacious trunk containing several disguises and a number of wigs, including one that I recognised: that of the red-haired Dr.Wickson.

That strange personage had thrown himself into a large leather armchair and had graciously invited the surrounding *gendarmes* to take a seat beside him.

He maintained an obstinate silence in the face of every question that M. Donneau put to him.

The examining magistrate asked me to show him the location of the secret door. I lifted up the tapestry and showed him a heavy oak door hidden behind it. As the prisoner refused to give him the key, the magistrate authorised it to be broken down and its hinges removed.

Once the door was down, thanks to the sturdy shoulders of the *gendarmes,* we were able to enter the murderer's cave.

I lifted up the loose tile and pulled out the large leather bag containing all the various objects I described previously.

The only things missing from the collection were the case containing the curare and the box of dissection instruments. M. Donneau ordered the skeleton to be brought to the centre of the room. Then he turned to Red Bomber and asked impatiently:

'Will you finally answer my questions and tell me when the skeleton was put in the cave?'

The bandit looked up.

'I'll tell you,' he said. 'It's the skeleton of M. Bréhat-Kerguen. I dissected it and prepared it myself, which provided Jacquot with an excellent meal. There isn't a single metal wire: all the ligaments are natural. It's a real anatomical triumph.'

He paused and turned to me.

'It surprises you to hear me confess, doesn't it, policeman? You're used to dealing with people whose every word has to be dragged out of them. Well, from now on, I shall reply to all your questions. I've made the decision: I shall tell you everything you want to know, down to the last detail. In any case, I have nothing to hide: everything I have done was for the best. And I'm growing tired of life. My father always told me I would die on the scaffold. Well, better that than elsewhere! To die in a public place, with the applause of the crowd, is better than to die in bed. Do you want to know how I introduced myself here; how I then went to Paris to claim the inheritance from my dear brother; how I found arsenic in his body; and how I had the honour to play cards with you at the Comtesse de Bréant's residence? Ask anything you want, and I'll tell you. But you have to admit I played the game well, and if the police hadn't assigned its rising star to the case, I would be living the good life: the sweetest life in the world.'

By now he was standing, and the words were rolling off his tongue, just like the charlatanism of Dr. Wickson.

At that point, the magistrate asked me to show him the room where the crime had taken place. I led him there; Red Bomber followed, escorted by five *gendarmes* pressing him closely. I had recovered the key to the room from Yvonne. As soon as I opened the door, and as soon as the killer realised that, after ten years, the room remained exactly the same as on the night of the murder, he could not suppress a shiver. He looked very troubled as he murmured:

'She told me everything had been put back in its place and the key had been lost.'

'Is this where you killed M. Bréhat-Kerguen?' asked M. Donneau.

Red Bomber said nothing, but nodded his head in agreement.

12

We left the Kerguen mansion yesterday morning at six o'clock. M. Donneau wanted to reach Locnevin before dawn, so as not to arouse the curiosity of the good people of Loc-ahr.

To cross the garden to reach the avenue, we had to go past Jacquot who was still tethered to the tree where he had been all night. He was growling loudly, but could not move without tearing his ear. He had a piteous air that Red Bomber seemed to find moving.

The prisoner asked his guards to stop for a moment so that he could say farewell to his old comrade.

'Goodbye, my poor Jacquot,' he said, tearing away the belt that tied the bear to the tree. 'Goodbye, my poor fellow. Your master is in quite a pickle, isn't he? What can you do, it all had to come to an end and this was inevitable. You can't understand that, can you? Because you're not lucky enough to be a rational creature. They're going to cut my head off, sooner or later, my old friend, and when I mount the scaffold you'll be amusing the crowd in a menagerie somewhere. You'll be well looked after, and well fed, and they'll give you cakes. Maybe you're lucky not to be a rational creature after all!'

I had also stopped, hands in pockets, to observe the touching scene, while M. Donneau went on ahead to make sure the wagon and horses would be ready to take us away.

Red Bomber looked quickly around and, leaning over Jacquot who was still lying in the snow, raised his steel handcuffs and dealt the bear a vicious blow on its spine, shouting:

'Have at them, Jacquot! Have at them! Revenge me!'

The bear let out a scream of pain and, raising itself on its rear legs, rushed towards me, its eyes blazing with fury.

Luckily at that moment I had hold of my pistols. I brought them out of my pockets in one swift movement and, just as the beast was getting ready to crush me in its terrible arms, I shot it point blank through its thick fur.

Jacquot dropped dead in the snow without a sound.

With a mighty curse, Red Bomber got up and started walking again.

At the sound of the double detonation, M. Donneau had turned round. He ran towards me, asking anxiously if I had been hurt. I pointed silently to the bear's corpse.

The poor *gendarmes* had been so stunned by the speed of events that they seemed not to hear the examining magistrate's loud reprimand of their carelessness towards the prisoner.

At the garden gate we found the carriage that M. Donneau had brought.

The magistrate bade me climb into the vehicle with him. He placed the prisoner between the five *gendarmes*. A rope passing under Red Bomber's arms was solidly attached to the saddles of the two strongest horses, and the men were under orders to fire on him if he attempted to escape. The little convoy advanced on foot, while M. Donneau and I took the lead in our shabby cabriolet.

When we arrived at the first houses of Loc-ahr, I asked the examining magistrate if we could stop the vehicle.

I stepped down in front of the modest thatched cottage where my little friend Jean-Marie lived, wrapped a few pieces of gold in my tie, and pushed in through a gap under the door.

After having thanked the poor child thus for his intelligent and devoted assistance throughout the affair, I climbed back next to the magistrate, who did not stop talking for the rest of the journey about our important capture and the honours his superiors were going to bestow upon him as a result of our unexpected success.

Two hours later, we entered Locnevin.

I asked to be put down at the Auberge de l'Ecu de France. As I took leave of M. Donneau, I asked that I be notified once the prisoner had been taken to his cell, and to allow me to participate in the interrogation.

The examining magistrate informed me that it would be his greatest pleasure to accede to my wishes.

'Besides,' he added, 'we can snatch a few more moments of rest, because the accused won't arrive at the town prison for another two hours and I can only interrogate him once the hearing has taken place, which won't be until about one o'clock in the afternoon.'

He took his leave of me to go back to court. I threw myself into an armchair and in no time at all I was asleep, because I was exhausted.

13

A few sharp knocks at my door aroused me from my slumber. The hearing was over and the examining magistrate, as promised, had sent someone to fetch me so that I might participate in the interrogation of Red Bomber.

When I arrived in the magistrate's chambers, the interrogation was already underway. M. Donneau was impatient to get to the bottom of this serious affair, which would surely enhance his growing reputation.

Two *gendarmes* were stationed in the corridor leading to the chambers. Two others had accompanied the prisoner inside. The unusual skill and forcefulness of Red Bomber had called for extraordinary precautions.

As I entered, M. Donneau greeted me with a friendly wave of the hand. The prisoner rose gravely and, turning towards me, said with the exaggerated courtesy that was his trademark:

'I owe you a thousand apologies, monsieur. I took you for a police agent, but I have just learnt that you are an amateur who takes pleasure in the manhunt, as others do with the hunting of wild animals. Now I know that, I consider you to be the most exceptional man I know and I sincerely regret my attempt to have you eaten by Jacquot. Poor Jacquot! It was no mean feat to capture me. Others have tried and failed, even at odds of twenty to one.'

The accused was interrupted at this point by the examining magistrate, who had become increasingly impatient and was anxious to get back to an interrogation that promised so many interesting revelations.

He ordered Red Bomber to sit down again.

'You promised this court not to conceal any of your crimes,' he continued, 'and to reveal the names of all your accomplices. Is that still your intention?'

'Forgive me, monsieur magistrate,' the accused replied with *sang-froid*. 'It's true that I promised you my life story. With regard to those whom you call my accomplices, it would be very difficult for me to name them all. For, even if I could remember all of them, there wouldn't be enough room in your prisons to hold everyone that had, directly or indirectly, helped me in my endeavours.

'My list would have to begin with the Governor General of the West Indies, who honoured me with his friendship after my escape from Cayenne, and end with the Countess of Bréant, at whose home I was privileged to play a game of cards with the gentleman here.

'I shall therefore limit myself to a brief summary of the principal passages of my life, giving only the salient features. I plan to provide the details in the Memoirs I intend to publish while I am in prison— unless I take it into my head to escape yet again.

'I hope to spare you the trouble of asking questions,' continued the accused, who obviously like long speeches—which showed how adroit he must have been to play the role of the taciturn Bréhat-Kerguen. 'I'll skip quickly over my early years so as to get to what seems to interest you most: my introduction into the mansion of the old wolf of Kerguen and my expedition to Paris to search for his brother's last will and testament.'

After this preamble, the accused started his story which turned out to be very long, lasting until seven o'clock at night.

I won't trouble you with all the details. The newspapers will certainly publish them all during the hearings, and you will be able to read how this cold-bloodedly audacious man managed to commit so many monstrous crimes without being caught.

He proved to us that it was his love of anatomy that had proved his undoing.

At the age of twenty-five, he was sent to prison in Cayenne for murder. At the time of his arrest there was insufficient proof against him, and he was about to be released when the carefully dissected arm of his victim was found in his room.

In the present case—which will probably cost him his life—if I hadn't noticed M. Bréhat-Kerguen's skeleton in the darkness of the cave; if I hadn't taken it into my head to do a search; if I hadn't found the leather bag; then the prick I had felt in my heel on Friday night would have been fatal and he would have escaped with impunity.

When the examining magistrate expressed astonishment that such an adroit and resourceful man would keep such a damning piece of evidence as the skeleton of his victim, he replied:

'I can't explain it, God knows. I was always telling myself I had to get rid of it. Once I carried it as far as the fish-pond to throw it in the water. But it seemed like an act of weakness: an act of cowardice that was beneath me. And I had prepared it so well! It was a veritable *objet d'art* that I liked to look at: I didn't want to get rid of it. It was like a trophy for my brilliant victory over the police: not only had I escaped from their clutches but I, who had been hunted like a wild beast; I, a bandit with a price on his head; I had installed myself in a feudal castle where I lived like a great lord!'

He then explained how he had managed to evade pursuit ten years earlier; how his knowledge of medicine, acquired in India after his escape from Cayenne, had enabled him to play the role of Dr. Wickson twice in the last ten years: a role which had opened doors to all the salons of Paris and allowed him to throw the police off his scent.

He was obviously an incredibly gifted man, but one whose talent was submerged by his audacity and *sang-froid*, with the result—to which you can attest from what you know of him—that intrepidness always won over finesse.

He has a considerable narrative talent and employs rich and vivid expressions of speech.

We listened to him as if we were in the Paris salons and he was a voyager returning from strange places and recounting his adventures with incomparable charm. He spoke enthusiastically of his crimes and seemed to be proud of them.

Were it not for the *gendarmes* surrounding him and the handcuffs tethering him, he could have been mistaken for a long-lost friend recounting his adventures abroad and the events of a long and perilous voyage, not for a prisoner accused of a capital offence whose head has already been promised to the scaffold.

The man's strong yet bizarre character interested me enormously, and now that the unfortunate Guérin is certain to go free, I find myself almost hoping that Red Bomber escapes the final justice. It would really be a tragedy for a man of such talent to end his life under the blade of the guillotine, like a common criminal.

I've selected those facts from the interrogation which are pertinent to what will one day be called *The Bréhat-Lenoir Affair*, and am sending you a brief summary in haste.

His confession with regard to the murder of M. Bréhat-Kerguen confirms Yvonne's account in every detail.

I asked him why, on Thursday night, he had tried to force his accomplice to leave for Rennes and why, when she refused, he decided to kill her.

'Ah!' he replied. 'I was reasonably certain you had come with me to spy on me and discover my secrets. I was not afraid of you on your own. I was also certain you would get nothing out of the old idiot, who by the way had no information to impart, given that he had never noticed that I took the place of his real lord and master.

'But I was afraid of Yvonne. As you know, women are subject to remorse and to nervous attacks. If you had become aware of her presence in the mansion—and what followed proved my fears were well-founded—you would have been able to get her to talk. That's why I wanted to send her to Rennes and why I wanted to kill her when she refused.'

'But why, once you had discovered who I was, didn't you get rid of me, as you had wanted to do with Yvonne?'

'I'll tell you. When you presented yourself to me in Paris, I took you for a veritable bumpkin, stupid and harmless, so good was your disguise. I was delighted to engage your services because I needed to arrange the deceased's possessions. I didn't want to use the steward Prosper because I was wary of his inquisitiveness and loose tongue; in addition, I had been in an encounter with a young diplomat two days before and my kidneys had been damaged, which prevented me bending down.

'So I took you into my service, fully expecting to send you back to the country once I left Paris.

'But I recognised you at the Comtesse de Bréant's *soirée* when you came to sit down opposite me. I recognised you by your eyes: they have a strange look I had already noticed and that evening they were almost frightening. When I found myself being examined with such fierce attention, and when I saw your long fingers counting out the cards one by one, I was almost afraid. Yes, I, Red Bomber, afraid! And I didn't dare cheat, I who wasn't afraid to play tricks under the nose of M. Ribeyrac, the public prosecutor, himself!

'I realised then that I was dealing with a formidable adversary, so in order to throw you off track I conceived an audacious project—too audacious as it turned out, for I should have foreseen the outcome. I decided to take you to Brittany with me and not to let you out of my sight for a minute until I could be sure whether you were a deadly enemy or not. Because of a thousand small details I quickly became certain you were, despite your expert disguise, no more fit to wear a servant's uniform than I was to wear a policeman's!

'I took you for an agent sent by the Paris Prefecture: that was my fatal mistake. I should have known that no employee from police headquarters could have demonstrated such skill and audacity. That skill was so extraordinary that I intended, once you arrived here, to seduce you with an offer a thousand times more generous than what I imagined your policeman's pay to be. I would have hired you and employed you on a vast project I planned to set in motion once I inherited the Bréhat-Lenoir estate, for which I needed a man of your ability. Such was my plan. I wanted your fate linked to mine—I felt a certain sympathy for you—and I told myself that, after all, you were in my hands and, at the slightest sign of trouble, I could get rid of you.

'It was under these circumstances that I received the letter from M. Berteau, the lawyer, who called me from Rennes to work out the details of the inheritance. I left in a great hurry, taking advantage of a moment when you were not spying on me. I had told old Yves to let you know I had shut myself in my room because I was not feeling well, and not to tell you I had gone away. How did you manage to get that idiot to talk?

'On my return, my first stop was the cave that you know about. I saw a footprint on the tiled floor that wasn't my own. I was shocked and surprised and vowed to kill you.

'But you showed your prowess once again when you scraped my needles and coated them with some innocuous concoction in the place of the curare.

'When you removed the leather case, you signed your own death warrant because, having been deprived of my favourite weapon, I had to revert to the dagger, which would not have been a simple pin-prick.'

14

'You must now tell us,' interrupted M. Donneau, 'how you conceived the idea of murdering M. Bréhat-Lenoir and how you carried it out.'

'It's very simple,' replied the prisoner, with his customary calm. 'I read in the deceased Bréhat-Kerguen's papers that he had an immensely rich brother living in Paris, and more recently I found correspondence that proved how strained relations were between the two brothers. From one of the letters I learnt that M. Bréhat-Lenoir intended to disinherit the Breton. But I only found the papers in the last three months. Until then, I had always believed that the man whose place I had taken had no living relatives. I looked for those papers for nine years in every nook and cranny of the mansion. Eventually I found them behind the large Venetian mirror in the armour room.

'I made a quick decision. I was less concerned about being disinherited and more interested in the many millions I would need to begin the great project I mentioned before, for which I hoped to enlist the gentleman here.

'So I left for Paris to search for the will that disinherited the person whose place I had taken. Once the will was effectively annulled, I would inherit without difficulty.

'I was well favoured by circumstance, for the old wolf of Kerguen never ventured out of his mansion: almost nobody had seen his face. It was therefore very easy for me to pass myself off as him. Also, I have always been—just like the gentleman here—adept at disguise. I was about the same height as the deceased; his great wig of tousled hair and his face like an unwashed bear were easy to copy, and since he never spoke a word I never had a problem imitating his voice.

'Once I reached Paris, I spent about a week studying M. Bréhat-Lenoir's habits and the layout of the house and surroundings. Even though he had retired from business, he went to the Stock Exchange every day from two to four, for amusement.

'I purchased a doorman's uniform and, carrying under my arm an artfully arranged newspaper and voluminous parcel, I arrived at the door of the house around three o'clock.

'I had carefully timed my visit to occur when M. Prosper was away, for I was wary of the little steward.

'The only person there was Guérin, loafing on the doorstep with his hands in his pockets.

'"M. Bréhat-Lenoir?" I asked.

'"He's not here," replied the naïve peasant, bowing and scraping.

'"I know he isn't," I continued, with a loud guffaw. "I asked that to make sure this is his house. He was the one who sent me here. He approached me outside the Stock Exchange—right by the wine merchant's, you know—and asked me to bring this package over and put it over the fireplace in his room. Could you please indicate where to find his room? It's a heavy parcel, and it's a long way from the Stock Exchange to here."

'Guérin accompanied me up the stairs and showed me his master's room, for which he had the key.

'I placed my false parcel on the mantelpiece.

'"Oh!" I said, turning round suddenly as if I'd just remembered something, and searching my pockets. "Here's a letter your master told me to give to you to take to this address right away. There's not a minute to lose. I didn't want to take it myself because it was too far out of my way. You'd better go quickly, or M. Bréhat-Lenoir will be very upset."

'I pushed him by his shoulders and he rushed down the stairs two at a time.

'I started by going to the window to see whether, in case of danger, I could escape from there. But there were solid bars on the window, so there was no lifeline there.

'Next, I took the paper that was supposedly the outer cover of the parcel, crumpled it up and threw it on the fire, then lay down under the bed to wait for a favourable moment.

'M. Bréhat-Lenoir normally went to bed at nine o'clock. I heard him scold Guérin for having dared to penetrate his room against his orders. The latter stammered an excuse in which the words "letter" and "parcel" occurred frequently. But since the banker had given no such order relative to letters and parcels, he became very angry with his servant and swore he would dismiss him the following day.

'One hour later, M. Bréhat-Lenoir received the terrible wound whose effect, as you know, was as if he had been struck by lightning.

'Once he was dead, I searched the writing desk.

'I forced it open in such a way as to leave obvious traces. I wanted it to look like the work of a burglar.

'In one of the secret drawers, I found the will, which I burned straight away. Then I dropped a few grains of arsenic in the cup standing on the table and went back under the bed.

'You can see that my plan was cleverly conceived.

'You know the confusion that reigned the following morning. I slipped out from under the bed amidst all the tumult. So many people were milling around the house that my presence was not noticed.'

'Your account is not quite accurate,' I said after the accused had finished describing his exploits, 'so I shall take the liberty of completing it.'

He looked surprised and shot me an anxious look.

'Certainly,' I continued. 'You have forgotten to mention that, fearful of being noticed, you came into the house at night and left there in the morning, not through the main door to the street, but by the little garden entrance from the Rue de Vaugirard and the path that runs alongside the Hotel du Renard Bleu.'

'I said I would hide nothing,' replied the accused with a sombre air, 'and I have left nothing out.'

'Apart from the name of one of your accomplices, Little-Dagger, who hid you in his room, thus enabling you to enter the Bréhat-Lenoir residence without being seen.'

The bandit stared at me in disbelief.

'Look here,' I said, showing him the letter fragment that M. Prosper had found behind the trunk. 'Do you recognise these signs?'

'But you're a wizard,' cried Red Bomber, turning pale. 'Who gave you that paper? I looked for it for hours and I was convinced I had burned it. How did you get hold of it, and how did you manage to decipher it?'

'The most challenging puzzles can always be solved,' I replied. 'You should at the very least have taken the precaution of changing your codes. The master key was found by V** ten years ago, which is how your early accomplices were found.'

'So fate is decidedly against me,' murmured Red Bomber in a quiet voice.

'I was writing to an old associate,' he continued, turning to me—as if he felt the need to justify his mistake in the face of my reproach. 'I was force to use the old codes. Someone knocked on the door just as I was finishing the letter and I forgot that scrap of paper. I was sure that I'd thrown it on the fire. How did you find it?'

The rest of interrogation merely confirmed all my conjectures and revealed nothing you don't already know.

I must add, however, that Yvonne died the day after Red Bomber was arrested. She was buried secretly at the foot of one of the beech trees in the farthest corner of the garden.

Epilogue

Here ends the tale of Maximilien Heller.

The following pages may appear to be of little interest to those who were only seeking in this book an amusing diversion for a few hours, and who feel that the outcome of this factual narrative has sufficiently satisfied their curiosity. We thought, however, that after having followed the truly prodigious accomplishments of this young man in saving, at the risk of his own life, that of an innocent man and, with rare courage, delivering the guilty party into the arms of the law, those of our readers that wished him success during his perilous struggle and applauded his triumph would perhaps be happy to know what happened to Maximilien the Misanthrope afterwards. That is what we shall try to do in a few words.

Immediately upon his return from Paris, M. Heller sent me a note announcing his return and asking me to come and see him: he wished, he said, to speak to me as soon as possible.

One can imagine with what alacrity I responded to his invitation. Two hours after receiving his letter, I was climbing the six floors of the house on Butte Saint-Roche, at the very top of which the philosopher's attic was perched.

The light was beginning to fade. I found Maximilien Heller in exactly the same position as on that famous night when, a month ago, I had paid him my first visit.

He was leaning back in his armchair, in front of a hearth in which lay two dying brands. A candle burned behind him on the table. Only his cat was missing to complete the scene. It had doubtless taken advantage of Maximilien's long absence to find a kinder master and more comfortable lodgings.

My first words were, naturally, to congratulate him on the remarkable courage of which he gave such ample proof, as well as the felicitous outcome of his adventure. He barely mustered a reply, except for a string of broken monosyllables; it was as if I was bringing up a long-forgotten affair that invoked unpleasant memories. I wasn't really surprised by the strange welcome, being very familiar with my friend's bizarre nature. I enquired after his health.

'I'm not getting any better,' he said, turning his head slightly. 'Still the fever and the insomnia.'

I took the candle and placed it on the mantelpiece, so I could better observe the philosopher's demeanour and get a better idea of his state of health.

I noticed, with as much surprise as satisfaction, that the thirty days of continuous fatigue, battle, and emotional stress, far from aggravating his condition, seemed to have wrought a change for the better. His eyes were more alert and his features were less pale and drawn than that evening when I had seen him for the first time. I could not resist making that observation. He shook his head and replied emphatically:

'No, no, I assure you I'm no better than I was a month ago. You're only saying that to reassure me. It's no use, doctor. I'm under no illusions: I know better than anyone else how much I'm suffering.'

I thought to myself:

"You can protest as much as you like, my unsociable misanthrope. I know you're coming back to life."

He continued:

'Pray forgive me for disturbing you, doctor: I felt too weak to come to you… and I prefer nobody knows I'm in Paris. Here's what I wanted to ask you: would you be good enough to return the papers I left with you before my departure, as quickly as possible? I need to sort them out.'

'They'll be here tomorrow,' I replied.

'Thank you.'

He reached into his greatcoat and pulled out a red wallet, seemed to hesitate a little, then, handing me a pile of yellowish papers, said:

'That poor devil who's in prison—you know, Guérin—must be at the end of his tether. Please make sure he gets this modest sum.'

'Ah, Maximilien,' I said, shaking his hand vigorously, 'how good you are.'

My words seemed to create a strong impression. He frowned, squirmed in his armchair, and murmured sulkily:

'No, I'm not good. I'm fair, that's all. The society of man, in which I am forced to live, has been responsible for this poor unfortunate enduring great hardship. I consider myself responsible to some degree for this collective fault, and I intend to make recompense to the best of my ability. Mine is a simple act, and I am astonished that it should provoke such admiration. Besides, I have more money, far more than I need to live. I can claim no merit in ridding myself of something which is of absolutely no use to me.'

Listening to this declaration, made in such a dismissive manner, I could not help but smile. It is well known that doctors, observers by profession, eventually acquire a keenness of eye that enables them to perceive the maladies of the soul as well as those of the body. It seemed to me that, at this moment, Maximilien lacked the frank sincerity that has forever been the distinctive characteristic and, at the same time, the badge of honour of the misanthrope. Obviously he was forcing himself to proclaim something that was not in his heart. He had not spoken in this manner a month ago. Then, his words were bitter, cold, and incisive. At that time, one sensed that his soul was revolted to its very depths; that he disdained humanity for its vices and its errors; and that all his fellow creatures should be subjected to the powerful hatred that was festering in his heart. Now, his tone was forced and declamatory. Listening to him, I was reminded of a bad actor in the provinces who, playing Alceste in The Misanthrope, inflates his cheeks and bangs the furniture with his fists and feet. In vain did Maximilien Heller try to conceal the change to his interior self; in vain did he try to pretend that he had preserved in all its severity the morose and sceptical character he had presented to me since our first encounter: he could not fool me. Sufferings and misfortunes unknown to me, or perhaps a great injustice that he had suffered, had hitherto planted in his soul the poison of hate and despair.

But, by the grace of God, the poison had just found its antidote. How, in the face of the glorious and comforting work that he had just accomplished, could he doubt man's generosity? How, in the face of the success with which God had crowned his efforts, could he not recognise the power and the beauty of Providence?

It is a law of psychology to which all men must submit, that makes us judge the universe based on the limited world where we ourselves live, and leads us to contemplate our peers through the prism of our own virtues and faults. Our eyes are constantly fixed on the secret mirror of our soul, and it is on the image that we see there that we base the image of others.

So it was obvious to me that, seeing himself so great, so noble, and so beautiful in the mirror of his own soul, Maximilien was forced to reconcile with his fellow man and with God. In raising himself in his own eyes, he had raised, by the same token, all of humanity.

We both fell silent for a moment. Then Maximilien stood up, took several steps towards me, and said:

'My dear doctor, this will undoubtedly be the last time that I shall have the pleasure of meeting you. It would be ungrateful on my part if I failed to thank you for the care you have given me and the services you have rendered me over the last month.'

'What does this mean?' I asked in surprise. 'Are you leaving Paris?'

'No,' he replied with a sad smile. 'On the contrary, I'm all the more determined to stay.'

Conscious of the fact that I was awaiting an explanation of his cryptic utterances, he continued:

'My precise intention is to avoid causing a spectacle at the forthcoming trial. I have no desire to become the hero of a *cause celebre*. I shall leave this house and this room tomorrow and I wish, I very much wish, that my friends never discover my future whereabouts.'

'But your testimony is necessary, nay, indispensable to the judges.'

'Not at all. As you well know, the murderer has confessed everything.'

'You can't prevent your name being mentioned in connection with this affair, in which you played a very significant part.'

'What do you know? Suppose, for example, that I gave M. Donneau, the examining magistrate, a false name? How would you know? Only one person in the whole world knows the whole truth, and that's you. I asked you to come here so as to ask you, on your word of honour, never to reveal my secret as long as I live.'

'I promise,' I said, shaking his hand. 'But once the trial is over and the culprit is punished; once the affair passes into oblivion, won't you allow your friends to find you? Is it an eternal farewell that we say tonight?'

I was overcome with emotion as I pronounced these words. I believe that Maximilien noticed and was himself affected by the interest I showed in him.

He grasped my hand and said, in a brusque voice that barely hid his feelings:

'If we should by chance meet some day, I would see you again with great pleasure.'

François Bouchard, alias Red Bomber, was executed on the 25th of March 1846 at Saint-Jacques gate, in the presence of an immense crowd.

A few months after that final and lugubrious episode of this story—in the first part of July—I was walking along the quay opposite the Hotel de la Monnaie when I thought I saw a familiar figure at the open air stall of an antique bookseller: a tall, slender individual of striking appearance, the upper part of whose face was hidden by the wide brim of a *bolivar* hat. Despite the lengths he was taking to conceal his face, I had no difficulty in recognising my old friend Maximilien Heller.

I blessed the good fortune that had led to the encounter. For several weeks I had been actively seeking him through many quarters of Paris.

The reason that I had been trying to contact the philosopher after such a short delay will be revealed later.

He was holding a dusty volume between his long fingers, and seemed to be examining it attentively. He had not seen me, and to make him look up I had to tap him on the shoulder.

Maximilien Heller did not appear to be surprised or embarrassed. He placed the book back on the stall, and shook my hand.

'Doctor,' he said, 'I'm happy to see that you recognise your old friends.'

'For my part,' I answered with a smile, 'I'm sorry to note that you appear to have completely forgotten yours. I've been standing here, next to you, and—.'

'Forgive me,' he replied quickly. 'I was lost in my research.'

'Philosophical research, no doubt?'

'No, no,' Maximilien protested, as if he wanted to expunge an unpleasant memory, 'I've left philosophy behind me. Now I've taken up history.'

'Ah!'

'Yes, I've started an important project about French historical monuments.'

'And your studies require you to take frequent trips?'

'You know how much I dislike leaving my home. I do not possess the soul of a voyager. The only trip I ever took with pleasure is the charming itinerary traced by Xavier de Maistre in Voyage Around My Room.'

'It seems to me, however, that if you content yourself with touring your room, you can't expect to encounter many points of view that can further the aims of your project.'

'I consult those who have taken the trouble to travel on my behalf. I consult their books.'

'You are wrong, my dear friend,' I replied in my sternest physician's voice. 'You are wrong to bury yourself in such a dismal hide-away. The Paris air won't do you any good, believe me. You need to spend a few months in the country, by the seaside, up north or down south, no matter which. There is no greater relaxation than to travel, and you are in dire need of relaxation. I haven't forgotten how beneficial your expedition to Brittany a few months ago was to your moral and physical well-being, however dangerous it may have been.'

He made a gesture of denial.

'Don't try to argue with me,' I continued lightly. 'My professional eye did not deceive me, and I can't tell you how much I was struck by the improvement I noted at the time. Look here, because we've had the good fortune to meet again, let's take advantage of it: let me take you away.'

'What do you mean?' he replied, recoiling so quickly it made me smile.

'Last year I discovered a delightful little village perched atop a cliff on the Normandy coast, where the only inhabitants are fishermen, and the virgin soil has not been tarnished by the foot of a single bourgeois Parisian. I spent several months of indescribable peace and calm there, and I'd like to take you with me to experience the profound sense of well-being.'

I could see that he found the proposition tempting, but he still tried to resist.

'No, no, it's out of the question,' he said, casting around for an objection. 'I can't interrupt the project I've already started. I'm in the first throes of composition, and you must realise—.'

'What's to stop you working there?'

'I can't take my reference library with me.'

'I've got something better than a library to offer. At a short distance from the village, there are the ruins of a feudal castle, of great historical interest. It's a remarkable specimen that has so far escaped the attention of archaeologists and should be a very fertile source of interesting and curious discoveries.'

'And what is the name of this castle?'

'Trelivan.'

He appeared to be searching his memory.

'The name will surely be unknown to you,' I continued. 'I doubt very much if any of your books makes mention of it. But the scholarly disdain doesn't detract from its merit, and I'm sure you'll find the ruins of the old manor of great interest.'

My entreaties were so insistent that he had no defence against them and no way to refuse my offer.

Three days later, we were *en route* for Mareilles. Back in those days, seemingly so long ago, the casino had not yet spread like a voracious leprosy to every beach in Normandy and Brittany. One could have walked sixty leagues along the cliff tops without seeing a single one of those ugly tents tethered by guy ropes to pegs planted in the shore, or any of those motley costumes strewn among the gorse and the kelp, which today signify, seemingly in every nook and cranny, the unwelcome presence of a "seaside spa."

The Paris *bourgeoisie* dared not venture beyond Boulogne or Saint-Cloud, and only artists or amateurs with strong nerves risked travelling to the shores of the ocean and the channel.

The weather was magnificent when we arrived in Mareilles that evening. We installed ourselves in the best inn in town, situated on a small promontory that provided a splendid panorama of the open sea.

Our arrival seemed to bewilder the innkeeper, who had never had guests of our standing. He asked where we came from. I told him we were Parisians. The honest Norman, who was wearing the traditional cotton cap of the region, gave us a shrewd look then shook his grey head.

'My Lord,' he said, 'I think you're making fun of us country folk You? Parisian? Not a bit of it. I know Parisians very well. I saw one ten years ago and he didn't look a bit like you. Parisians have pointed hats like steeples, hair down to their knees, velvet garments and they carry a large box on the back.'

The peremptory assertion made me smile. He must doubtless have seen some amateur dauber one bright day, looking for a scenic view, and he imagined anyone coming from Paris would be wearing the romantic style of the 1830s. The sober and somewhat severe professional clothes that I was wearing clearly did not accord with his ideas. However, Maximilien, who appeared just at that moment wearing a tall hat perched on his long hair, set the innkeeper's mind at rest.

'There you are!' he exclaimed as soon as he saw him. 'That one's a real Parisian, Lord bless us!'

He put us up in a self-contained part of the building, which formed a pavilion.

Every day, from the next morning forward, we took a long walk along the cliffs to work up an appetite for lunch.

It seemed as though Providence conspired with me in favour of my poor, interesting friend. The sky was blue, the sun was hot and invigorating; the sea extended as far as the eye could see, its transparent waters punctuated here and there by white sails which the wind blew forward like frightened seagulls. The fresh air of the morning brought the sharp, clean odour of the sea to our nostrils. Our lungs drank in the healthy air in deep gulps as if they could never be completely assuaged.

I watched Maximilien out of the corner of my eye, all the while discussing botany, fishing, natural history and many other topics of interest. I noted with an inexpressible pleasure the salutary effects of the regimen I had imposed on him. His cheeks, exposed to the freshness of the wind, regained their youthful colour, so long absent. He walked with jaunty steps. His black hair rustled by the wind, his large eyes, sparkling with an unaccustomed brightness, were raised to the sky, giving his already striking appearance a touch of beauty.

I felt at that moment the joy that a gifted gardener must feel when he sees a small tree, hitherto bent under the devouring blast of the Mistral, straightening slowly and displaying a new coat of green finery.

For two weeks, we started each day with these invigorating excursions in the fresh air. Occasionally Maximilien enquired, as we were about to set off:

'Well, doctor, is today the day we're going to visit the ancient ruins?'

Each time he asked me the question, I found an adroit pretext to delay the start of our project. As the reader has no doubt long suspected, the ancient manor of Trelivan has only ever existed in my imagination, and I would have been mightily embarrassed if Maximilien had pressed the point. Happily he did not insist and each morning, by common consent, we deferred the excursion to the following day.

Eventually, towards the end of the third week of our stay in Mareilles, I said:

'Do you feel you have the strength, my dear friend, to undertake our expedition to the ruins of Trelivan? I warn you ahead of time that the whole journey will take us at least six hours there and back.

'Let's go!' he replied, with a youthful enthusiasm that I found charming. 'You must know by now that I'm a good walker and I don't tire easily.'

We descended the steep slope, at the summit of which sits the pretty village of Mareilles and, with our back to the sea, we struck out inland.

As soon as we left Mareilles, a small peasant could be seen at a hundred or so paces in front of us, running with his clogs in his hand and not turning to look at us. Maximilien failed to notice that we followed exactly the same path that the little guide took, and kept exactly the same distance between us.

After about half an hour of rapid walking, and after having followed charming shaded paths and traversed lush green fields, we arrived at a deep cutting in the hills, its dark recesses illuminated by dappled sunlight.

At a turning in the path we suddenly saw, in the midst of a clearing, a spacious farm house whose freshly whitened walls shone in the sunlight, behind a curtain of elegant poplars.

The little peasant disappeared behind a thick dogwood bush.

'Come,' I said to Maximilien, indicating the farm. 'If you like, we can make a brief stop here. The sun is terribly hot today, and we shouldn't turn our noses up at a glass of fresh milk.'

'I'm game,' he replied. 'That farm looks very tempting.'

We traversed a courtyard where fat ducks were waddling around and white chicken were clucking, and climbed the five steps leading to the dilapidated front door of the farm.

Just as I was about to raise the knocker, the door opened abruptly.

Maximilien gasped in surprise and teetered backwards a few steps.

'Jeanne! Jeanne!' cried a man's breathless voice, choking with emotion. 'Come quickly! He's here!'

A peasant some thirty years of age stood at the door, his face as red as a peony, laughing and crying at the same time. He clapped his large hands, turning first towards us then towards the inside of the house, repeating the words with an uncontrollable joy:

'Jeanne! I told you he would come. Hurry up! Ah, the Lord is good! Jeanne! Jeanne!'

'Louis Guérin,' murmured Maximilien, paling slightly.

Then he turned to me, smiled, and said with a sigh:

'Now I understand everything.'

Meanwhile Louis Guérin, for it was indeed he, had descended the stone steps. Overcome with an understandable feeling of gratitude, the honest fellow flung himself on his knees in front of Maximilien Heller and took hold of his hand, which he proceeded to kiss fervently while smothering it with his tears.

'It's you!' he repeated. 'You who saved me!'

'Get up my friend, I beg of you,' said Maximilien looking down at Guérin with a smile in his eyes.

'Calm yourself, Guérin,' I interjected. 'Calm yourself and introduce us to your wife.'

The peasant got up, wiped his red eyes, crossed the threshold and disappeared into the house.

Once we were alone, I turned to Maximilien who seemed to be making a great effort to hide the emotion that he felt.

'Well?' I asked.

He shook my hand, turning his head a little, then uttered two short words:

'Thank you.'

Guérin soon reappeared, accompanied by a young and pretty peasant of eighteen years, holding her hand in his.

She came towards us, blushing and with her eyes down.

Guérin made a sign for her to step forward and make a gesture that they had obviously prepared for some time.

But Jeanne just stood there, blushing even more furiously and not daring to speak.

Then, suddenly, she took hold of herself, stepped towards Maximilien, and with charming grace and *naïveté*, offered him one fresh young cheek, on which the philosopher—who had, I swear, completely shed his air of timidity—planted two hearty kisses.

Since the first expression of joy and gratitude, Guérin had calmed down somewhat, so I asked him if we could visit his charming property.

He took his wife's arm in order to steady himself, for his legs were still shaking, and together they showed us all their riches: the manger, where two magnificent cows were solemnly ruminating; the courtyard with its noisy inhabitants; the milking shed; the pressing shed where an immense vat was awaiting the next apple harvest, and all the other inestimable assets that he owed to the generosity of Maximilien Heller.

During the whole time he never stopped expressing his fervent gratitude to my friend in the most touching way. He interrupted himself frequently, during the enumeration of his assets and his plans for the future, to declare:

'And when I think that it is to you that I owe everything... My God! Without you what would I have become?'

Then he buried his head in his hands as the grim memory of his arrest and his nights in prison came back to him like a terrifying ghost.

Seeing these modest possessions, and listening to the naive expression of a happiness so joyful and so pure, I thanked God from the bottom of my heart for inspiring in Maximilien Heller such generosity and devotion.

There was no doubt that Maximilien shared the same emotion that I felt, for on his smiling face was an expression of happiness that I had never seen there before.

As we were returning to the farm along a narrow path, with the young peasant and his wife walking in front of us with intertwined arms, Maximilien stopped suddenly and took my hand which he shook vigorously. With a voice full of emotion, even tearful, he said:

'Ah, my friend! That gives me a good feeling! I, too, wish to thank you, for you have saved me!'

Postscript:
Clayton Rawson on Carr's Locked Room Lecture

There is another reason why *The Killing Needle* is historically important.

Clayton Rawson, magician, founding member of *The Mystery Writers of America* and author of numerous impossible crime novels and short stories, often engaged in friendly rivalry with John Dickson Carr. For example, In *Death from a Top Hat,* Chapter XIII, Rawson's detective, The Great Merlini, is critical of Dr. Fell's celebrated Locked Room Lecture from *The Hollow Man/The Three Coffins,* claiming that Fell mentioned two major classes of impossible murder method, but overlooked a third.

According to Merlini, Fell cited class A: "The crime that is committed in a hermetically sealed room which really is sealed, and from which no murderer has escaped, because no murderer was actually in the room," and class B: "The crime that is committed in a room which only appears to be hermetically sealed, and from which there is some more or less subtle means of escape."

After listing the sub-categories in each class, Merlini triumphantly announces that "there is one more class of flim-flam. Class C." He goes on: "Class C includes those murders which are committed in a hermetically sealed room which really is hermetically sealed, and from which no murderer escapes, not because he wasn't there, but because he stays there, hidden until *after* the room has been broken into, and leaves *before* it is searched." These words were written in 1938, Carr's lecture having been published in 1935.*

Although there is no grand denouement, and the solution is glossed over very quickly, it nevertheless remains true that the solution offered in 1871 in *The Killing Needle* is a perfect example of Rawson's Class C, and almost certainly the very first in the history of detective fiction.

JMP

149

*One could argue that the seventh sub-category in Class A, wherein the victim is actually alive but is killed by the first-in, is actually an example of Class C, because the murderer stays in the room—hidden in plain sight.

CPSIA information can be obtained
at www.ICGtesting.com
Printed in the USA
LVHW080221230522
719466LV00010B/405